'I suppose you

'No! Don't go.' Sue h
if to detain him, ther
smile.

'Am I forgiven so easily, then?' Edwin's smile became teasing. 'Now that I do find surprising. I quite expected to be given my marching orders, particularly as you've made it clear that you're immune to my obviously less than fatal charms!'

Dear Reader

With the worst of winter now over, are your thoughts turning to your summer holiday? But for those months in between, why not let Mills & Boon transport you to another world? This month, there's so much to choose from—bask in the magic of Mauritius or perhaps you'd prefer Paris... an ideal city for lovers! Alternatively, maybe you'd enjoy a seductive Spanish hero—featured in one of our latest Euromances and sure to set every heart pounding just that little bit faster!

The Editor

A born romantic, **Kristy McCallum** is lively, fun-loving and happily married to a very good-looking man. She has three children, three cats, one dog and other animals she adores. She lives in a particularly beautiful part of the West Country but it rains quite often, so travel to the sun features prominently in her plans. She hopes her readers share her belief that that special man should be kind, amusing and sexy, and passionately in love with her.

Recent titles by the same author:

DRIVEN BY LOVE

PAST IMPERFECT

BY
KRISTY McCALLUM

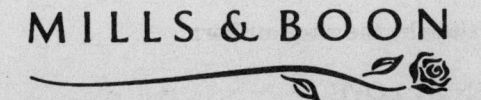

MILLS & BOON

MILLS & BOON LIMITED
ETON HOUSE, 18-24 PARADISE ROAD
RICHMOND, SURREY TW9 1SR

All the characters in this book have no existence outside the imagination of the Author, and have no relation whatsoever to anyone bearing the same name or names. They are not even distantly inspired by any individual known or unknown to the Author, and all the incidents are pure invention.

All Rights Reserved. The text of this publication or any part thereof may not be reproduced or transmitted in any form or by any means, electronic or mechanical, including photocopying, recording, storage in an information retrieval system, or otherwise, without the written permission of the publisher.

This book is sold subject to the condition that it shall not, by way of trade or otherwise, be lent, resold, hired out or otherwise circulated without the prior consent of the publisher in any form of binding or cover other than that in which it is published and without a similar condition including this condition being imposed on the subsequent purchaser.

First published in Great Britain 1994 by Mills & Boon Limited

© Kristy McCallum 1994

*Australian copyright 1994
Philippine copyright 1994
This edition 1994*

ISBN 0 263 78496 7

*Set in Times Roman 10½ on 12 pt.
01-9405-50994 C*

Made and printed in Great Britain

CHAPTER ONE

THE auctioneer cleared his throat and took a sip of water.

'Lot ninety-one. A watercolour by John Tamerton, signed and dated eighteen hundred and eighty-four. Who will start me? Yes? I am bid two hundred pounds... Two hundred and fifty... Three hundred...'

Susan Rivers tried not to hold her breath, tried to breathe normally, as she held up her catalogue, then nodded as the auctioneer, his attention caught, returned again and again to her as the bidding mounted.

'Nine hundred and fifty pounds... One thousand pounds.' Fiercely disappointed, she bit her lip, then decisively shook her head.

'One thousand pounds... I have been bid one thousand pounds?' There was a short silence, then the gavel fell with a sharp finality. 'Lot ninety-one sold to the gentleman at the back... Lot ninety-two...'

Susan turned round to search for the face she'd come to associate with her disappointment. Dark and saturnine, he was looking down at his catalogue, his glossy black hair catching the light, intent and oblivious to her attention, until he looked up quickly and caught her watching him. At once the brown eyes narrowed and he held her glance as the sale of Victorian pictures continued without their active participation.

It was with a mounting sense of panic that she wrenched her eyes away from his. He was here again! This time she'd been so sure she'd have little competition, apart from the dealers, and she knew most of them, so that it had come as a bitter disappointment to hear herself outbid yet again.

The platinum-blonde of her hair was cut in a bob that framed her face so naturally one couldn't imagine it arranged in any other way. Just now it fell forward, hiding her eyes and her mouth, both shadowed with disappointment. Normally lively, and full of expression, her eyes were set under long, gracefully curving lids, and were sufficiently unusual to draw most people's attention to them.

It was her mouth, though, with its full lower lip, that gave her such an air of brooding sensuality. She was under few illusions that it was her looks that had helped her with the dealers. They had been remarkably kind to a man, helping her inexperienced attempts over the last year to buy any of John Tamerton's work that came to their attention, and it was the dealers who acted as her unofficial guides and mentors. No work by him was offered for sale in the West Country without her being aware of it; indeed their network extended across the whole country.

While she didn't aspire to the big oils which were way beyond her pocket, she had managed to pick up half a dozen watercolours fairly reasonably until the advent of the unknown bidder who had managed with perfect ease to outbid her every time these last six months. She'd lost the chance to own three pictures— one that was particularly special because it portrayed the part of the village in Sussex where her family had owned a cottage in the last century.

Infuriatingly she still didn't know who he was, except that he was from London and was apparently seen at the grander sales which so far she'd always been too frightened to attend. Des, her main informant, was a runner for one of the bigger London galleries that specialised in eighteenth-century marine artists. Because their interests were never likely to clash he had appointed himself as her minder. Once she'd got used to his bizarre taste in clothes and yobbo hairstyle she'd found him a fund of useful information. It never ceased to surprise her that he knew so much about the Victorian painters and their work, in spite of his own different interests.

'Bad luck, girl!' Des came and slid into the empty seat next to hers. 'I really thought you were going to get lucky this time...'

'Yes, so did I!' she agreed bitterly. 'I wish I knew why he's so interested in John Tamerton's work. He must have arrived late because there was no sign of him earlier; I checked.'

'I've done a bit of research on him for you...' He smiled into her suddenly interested eyes. 'He's called Edwin Ashley and he owns the Ashley Gallery in London; that's in Belgravia by the way. The lucky so-and-so inherited it from his uncle, a nice old boy who was very well liked in the trade. This chap seems to be doing all right so far. He's got his interests, and they seem to be the same as yours... The word's out that he's interested in Tamertons, so unless you want to match his prices I don't think you're going to get lucky any more. He was also intrigued by you. Wanted to know if any of us knew why you were buying Tamerton's work as well.'

Susan bit her lip, then forced herself to remember how kind Des had been. 'Don't spread it around, but he's... well, family.'

'Family?' Des's eyebrows shot up.

'Keep your voice down...' she tried to shush him.

'What connection?' She didn't really blame him for his curiosity; she knew that was the basis for all his considerable knowledge about paintings and their artists.

'He was my great-grandfather, but I'd rather you kept quiet about it.'

Des gave a low whistle. 'No wonder you're interested... Have you more at home?'

Susan shook her head decisively. 'No. That's why I was trying to buy some back. My father—well, he's dead now so I suppose it doesn't matter to talk about it——' She broke off, a little doubtful about the wisdom of continuing her life story to someone who was a relative stranger.

'Well? Go on, you can't stop now!'

Looking at Des's face, she almost laughed. His rather long, inquisitive-looking nose was almost twitching as she kept him in suspense.

'My father was a gambler. He died a bankrupt so nearly everything went. He had to sell all his grandfather's pictures.'

Des let his breath out in a long sigh. 'That's bad, girl... Didn't he leave you anything?' By now Susan was definitely regretting confiding in him. She shook her head.

'Not a thing!' Then she smiled. 'So, now you know why I'm interested in John Tamerton.'

Des's expression had become closed and uninformative, and Susan guessed he was thinking something out. He looked like this sometimes when he was bidding. 'You were lucky, then, weren't you, that that Ashley chap didn't come on the scene a bit earlier?'

Once more she bit her lip, then she shrugged slightly. 'I suppose that's one way of looking at it, certainly.'

'You got half a dozen watercolours at a very competitive price, didn't you? You could make a bit of profit by selling one or two of them on, you know. Would you like me to act for you?'

'Sorry, Des. I'm not in the business of dealing, as I thought you understood.'

'Come on, girl! No one's above making an honest penny these days.'

'No, I suppose not, but you see I don't want to sell. It doesn't look as if I'll ever be able to buy in any more of John Tamerton's work at a price I can afford, so I must just be grateful for what I have.'

'Shame!' He gave her a quick smile. 'I'll miss seeing you around...'

'And I'll miss you!' she agreed warmly, thankful at having been allowed off the hook.

'Do you want me to continue doing any more research? Like is he buying for himself or a customer?'

She flushed, once more a little unhappy about having doubts about his motives. It wasn't so much what he said, as what lay behind his words. She sensed he wanted her to agree, to keep in touch with him.

'No, I don't think so, do you? There wouldn't be much point as far as I'm concerned because I've shot my bolt. No, I'll call it a day, and just be grateful for what I've managed to collect.' She stood up, as the auctioneer took a small break before continuing the sale. Des let her pass him, then followed her out into the small ante-room that was full of dealers smoking and chatting to each other as they waited for their lots to come up.

'It's been really nice meeting you, Des, and I wish you all the luck in the future...'

'You're throwing in the towel?'

She tried to ignore the scorn in his voice, and gave him a deprecating smile. 'I'm not a wheeler and dealer by nature, and I'm happy to let things stand as they are.'

'Why don't you let me take on this geezer for you?'

'No, Des, there'd be no point, would there? I haven't the money to take him on, and nor have you!' Once more she saw the blank, uncommunicative look on his face as he wrestled with some inner problem. 'Look, you've been more than kind, and I'm very grateful, but it couldn't last forever, could it? I reckon I've been lucky to get hold of six watercolours, so it's goodbye, I'm afraid...' She held out her hand and waited for him to take it. He did so, reluctantly, and she smiled. 'Maybe I'll see you around, but for the moment I don't think I'll be attending any more sales.' She gave him a brisk smile, trying to ignore the faint speculation she saw in his eyes, before turning away and making for the car park.

She was so busy thinking about her own disappointment that she was quite oblivious to anything happening around her.

'Hey! Why the hurry? I've been wanting to meet you for a very long time...' The voice, low and sexy, stopped her dead in her tracks as she looked up, startled, to meet the eyes of the stranger who had just outbid her. Confident assurance was implicit in every arrogant line as he looked down at her, the mouth widely generous, with lips tilted upwards in amusement, as he took in her affronted expression. 'Oh, dear! You don't look very pleased, but business is business, you know, and it really isn't a personal matter.'

Now Sue wasn't at all sure she liked the way he had lingered over the word 'personal', and he was taking a great deal for granted. Just because he behaved as if most women fell on their knees before him, there was no need at all for her to follow suit. So, OK, he was a pretty charismatic-looking man, but this wasn't the first time he'd managed to spoil her day, oh, no! She kept her face set in non-committal lines.

'Yes?' There was a definite warning behind the *froideur*, and the dark stranger's eyes began to dance with wicked amusement.

'I'm so very sorry——' his voice was a parody of upper-class manners '—we haven't been introduced, have we? My name is Edwin Ashley, and at the moment I'm very interested in acquiring John Tamerton's work. I believe you share my—er—interest in the gentleman?'

'So?' She raised her eyebrows in faint surprise, and just for a moment was pleased to see that he looked slightly disconcerted.

'Look, I'm sorry I've managed to outbid you the last few times. If you'd tell me who you're working for, maybe we could join forces?'

Sue continued to look at him, a considering expression on her face.

'I don't suppose you're sorry at all; after all, you've just said "business is business".' He had the grace to look a little rueful as he stuffed his hands into the pockets of his well-cut jeans. 'Anyway, I'm not working for anyone...'

He looked amazed. 'You're buying for yourself?'

'What's wrong with that?' she enquired stiffly.

'Why, nothing, nothing at all. It's just...' He spread his hands a little helplessly. 'You don't look as if you specialise in collecting Victorian art.'

'I don't!' she agreed pleasantly. 'Now, if you'll excuse me...' A warm hand was placed on her arm.

'Look, please don't go! Anyway, you haven't told me your name, or anything about you!'

Affronted at his audacity, she treated him to one of her fiercest frowns.

'Why on earth should I tell you anything about me?' she demanded. 'For a start you're a stranger, and I know nothing about you.'

'Funny. I thought that odd-looking chap sitting next to you was filling you in with all the details!' he attacked, and Sue's face flamed with colour.

'Look, I'm not in the mood for being picked up, so why don't you leave me alone?' A couple of passing dealers, after nodding to the dark man, gave the two of them interested looks.

'Do you want to ruin my reputation?' A look of humour was on his face. 'That lot'll never let me forget

I nearly got my face slapped by some blonde in a car park!'

'Why don't you take the hint, then?' Sue smouldered, trying to control her anger. This was the man who'd just outbid her yet again, and here he was, chatting her up and making a joke about it!

'Now you're angry!' The dark eyes looked concerned as he studied her face. 'I didn't mean to upset you. Look, here's my card! I run a perfectly respectable gallery in the West End of London. If you feel like calling in for a chat any time, then do so. I've got some nice Tamertons there at the moment...' Once more his face creased up with amusement. 'You're quite a girl, aren't you? Don't worry! I shan't bother you again, at least not until I can find someone respectable who'll vouch for me! He gave her a devastating smile before turning away, and on now slightly unsteady legs Sue continued on her way, determined not to show that he was anything but a chance-met stranger, and one she didn't particularly care to meet again.

As she started her small runabout she was conscious of a faint feeling of relief that he'd let her go so easily; just for a moment back there she'd been worried he might have been trouble. All the same, as she drove home to the small village in Devon where she now lived she was conscious of a niggling resentment against Edwin Ashley. It seemed so unfair that this stranger should have been able to outbid her so easily, and what spirit of perversity had made her repel the advances of what had to be one of the most attractive men she'd met in a very long time?

She walked back into her cottage hoping that Bridget would still be there. Although officially retired from work when Sue's grandmother had died, she still liked to come in and potter around, and Sue, who had known her most of her life, was always happy to see her.

'Well? Have you found out who your mystery man is?' Bridget took a lively interest in all Sue's affairs.

'Yes, at least Des found out for me. He's called Edwin Ashley and owns a gallery in London.'

'A London man coming down all the way to the West Country for a relatively unimportant sale?'

'Perhaps he prefers to do his own buying; Des told me he's a comparative new boy to the trade.' Bridget looked her interest. 'Apparently he inherited the gallery from an uncle,' Sue continued, slightly unwillingly, knowing that Bridget wouldn't rest until she'd extracted the last detail.

'Do you know where it is?'

'Oh, yes. Des gave me all the information. Anyway, Edwin Ashley tried to pick me up afterwards, and gave me his card.' She tried to speak in an offhand manner, as if the encounter were unimportant, because Bridget was quick at picking up her unspoken thoughts.

'Still pining for that ex-boyfriend of yours?' The older woman sniffed. 'It's about time you forgot all about him and found someone to take his place!'

'Yes, Bridget!' Sue smiled at this advice, which was given regularly.

'Des becoming a problem?' Bridget enquired shrewdly, and Sue shrugged.

'I don't know... Could be, I suppose. I told him John Tamerton was my great-grandfather. He wanted me to sell some of my pictures to make a quick profit. I think he was disappointed that I wouldn't play.'

'I can't think why you're surprised. After all, that's what he does all the time. He probably thought you were mad to turn him down.' It was Susan's turn to laugh and she did so, not even pretending to disguise her relief.

'Of course! I should have realised I just wounded his pride. I suppose, even though I told him he was family, he still couldn't believe I wasn't interested in making a profit.'

'Sue, you didn't tell Des or that Ashley man that you paint, did you?'

'Now Bridget! I might be an idiot in your eyes, but at least I knew that really would put the cat among the pigeons!'

'All the same, if this man Ashley owns a number of Tamertons it might be interesting to go up and have a look in his gallery, wouldn't you think?'

Sue wasn't fooled for a minute. 'It's time you went home, Bridget, and you can safely leave me alone to find another man in my life without encouraging me to pick up strangers outside auction rooms! But if it makes you happier, I've already decided I'll have to go and see just what he's managed to get hold of, because it's extraordinary that he should be known to be interested in any Tamertons that come on to the market. There has to be a reason behind it.'

'Maybe he's planning to hold a what-you-call-it, that thing I read in the papers the other day...'

'A retrospective?'

'That's it!'

'Could be. I think its more likely that he's buying for someone else.'

Bridget gave her a quick look. 'I see...' Then she smiled. 'I think you should tell him who you are! That you're John Tamerton's great-granddaughter, and that you've inherited his talent!'

'Now that's not true and you know it!' Sue protested. 'My only real skill seems to lie in the fact that I can copy, and I can't believe John Tamerton would have approved of that!'

'Why not? You earn a living and the insurance companies love you.' She wrinkled her nose, but as Bridget made ready to leave she let it pass.

All the same, alone in her room that night Sue couldn't get the image of Edwin Ashley out of her mind. That face with its dark good looks seemed to take on the power of an avenging angel as he dominated her thoughts.

She tried to give herself a rational talking-to about getting obsessed with a perfect stranger, but he'd appeared in her life with all the dramatics of a demon king, thwarting her wishes with such contemptuous ease that she found it impossible to dismiss his image lightly.

Something had been niggling at the back of her mind all evening, something that Des had said to her... Of course! Edwin Ashley was apparently interested in finding out about her. Now, how did Des know that unless he was in closer contact with Mr Ashley than he'd told her?

Once more she silently berated herself for allowing Des to get beneath her guard. It had been stupid to tell him of her relationship to John Tamerton, particularly because—— But here she broke off her thoughts abruptly. Next week she was due in London to deliver the first of four copies of Victorian London scenes that had been commissioned by a city company to hang in its boardroom. She would certainly make time to visit Edwin Ashley's gallery, and, if he recognised her, so what? Surely she was capable of handling their meeting in a rational and adult manner? Satisfied, she now rolled over in bed and determinedly prepared to sleep.

The Ashley Gallery was imposing enough in a quiet way, Sue found as she stopped in front of the window to admire a rather beautiful painting by Dudley Hardy of a couple of old fisherwomen sorting out the catch on a beach. The subdued colours of their old clothes contrasted sharply with the glittering scales of the mackerel and sprats that tumbled out of great baskets in front of them. It was a large watercolour and the artist in her responded with appreciation as she studied its compulsive appeal.

'It's unusually good, isn't it?' a voice said next to her. 'Of course his output was varied, and he worked as an illustrator and cartoonist among other things, but I think this particular example is quite exceptional.'

'It's beautiful,' she agreed, but suddenly realising whom she was talking to had her turning, disconcerted, to look straight into Edwin Ashley's face. Warm sherry-brown eyes looked back at her, a hint of amusement just beginning to curl the edges of that firm-lipped, generous mouth.

'I'm very pleased to meet you, Miss Susan Rivers! Now——' a firm hand was placed under her elbow '—why don't you come into my gallery and be introduced to some of your great-grandfather's work that I've been privileged to acquire over the last couple of years?'

Susan found that she was prey to a peculiar weakness that allowed her to appear to give in gracefully, because she didn't know how else to explain to herself afterwards the ease with which she allowed him to lead her into his gallery.

'Georgina!' he called, and Sue noticed a rather horse-faced girl get up from the rather ornate desk that dominated their immediate surroundings.

'Edwin!' She walked over gracefully to join them, a professional smile curling her lips, but Sue noticed that the smile didn't reach her eyes, which were coolly assessing her and her ability to buy any of the pictures that lined the walls. She was tall and elegant and Sue immediately felt like a country frump as she took in the expensive and beautifully understated clothes. Cross with herself, she raised herself to her full height of five feet four inches, unaware that that made her look about as aggressive as a bantam hen ready to defend its chicks. She felt even crosser when she saw Edwin Ashley slant an amused look at his assistant.

'This is Susan Rivers, John Tamerton's great-granddaughter.' Sue knew Edwin was perfectly aware that she had gone into defensive mode. All this absurd formality on his part had to be a form of punishment because she'd refused to succumb to his blandishments outside the auction rooms the week before. 'Miss Rivers, I'd like you to meet Georgina Foliot...'

She stiffened slightly as the other girl's expression changed to one of amused interest.

'Goodness! Is this Des's little girlfriend?'

Sue found herself biting down hard on her teeth at the upper-class voice that was so neatly trying to label her as 'not one of us'. Still, she wasn't one to give in without a fight.

'Des?' She turned to give Edwin Ashley a blank look. 'Who's Des?'

He laughed. 'Oh, come on! Surely you know Des? He's that chap who was sitting next to you at the sale last week.'

She pretended to frown slightly, then her brow cleared. 'I suppose you mean that extraordinary-looking man who hangs around the sale rooms?' she queried with a frown. 'I think he has to be the only Des I've ever encountered, although I can hardly claim him as a friend. Mind you, he's been kind to me, but then I've found most of the dealers I've met have been kind to me!' she finished with a sly, mischievous smile.

'I'm sure they have!' Edwin gave her an admiring look. 'You must have found it a great asset.' His own eyes were making it clear that he, too, could see exactly what it was about her that interested the dealers, but Georgina's face, as she gave her boss an indulgent look, made Sue feel a little uncomfortable, almost as if she'd been, in some subtle way, put down.

'I did until you came along and started to outbid me!' she agreed, with a return of her frosty manner.

'Yes...I suppose you must have found my entrance on to a the scene a bit disconcerting.' Sue gave him a tiny smile.

'Oh, I'm not really complaining. I suppose I've had a very good run for my money, and consider I've done very well to get as many pictures as I have.' Edwin's eyes had narrowed.

'Hmm. How many John Tamertons do you own?' His voice was deceptively quiet, as if he had no real interest in her answer, but Sue was not to be fooled. She raised her eyebrows slightly.

'I don't want to disappoint you, Mr Ashley, so let's get something straight from the start. None of them is for sale!'

'I can understand that, particularly with your family history, but...' But Sue had had enough for her inquisition, so she moved over to look at a large oil depicting a biblical scene.

'This is very fine. Is it by John William Waterhouse?'

'I see you've studied your Victorian artists!' He walked over to join her, followed by the supercilious Georgina, who took over the conversation.

'Yes, it is actually. One of his better pictures... And this particularly fine family group is by Singer Sargent. It's an attractive composition, isn't it? Of course this particular study is particularly noted for the fine play of light and shade on the subjects...' She continued in this practised manner, showing all the pictures, but with an air of lecturing someone ignorant of the finer points of the artists concerned, which Sue found intensely irritating.

Edwin seemed content to step back and let her take the limelight, and Sue couldn't help wondering if that proved they worked as a team, or had a closer relationship. All the same she found it disconcerting in the extreme to discover that he was studying her as intently as any painting. She was still wary as, towards the end of the impromptu lecture, Edwin interrupted.

'Thanks, Georgina. Now I'll take Miss Rivers downstairs to see the Tamertons. I'm sure we'll all be grateful for one of your delicious coffees when we return...' Smoothly, he led the way down the red-carpeted stairs to the lower level of the gallery, and Sue was forced to revise her opinion of him, as she saw Georgina's momentarily unguarded expression. She might try to act as if she were equal partners with the boss, but it seemed Edwin Ashley was quite capable of putting her in her place if he felt like it. This thought gave her quite disproportionate pleasure as she followed him down the stairs, and the pleasure was compounded as her mouth fell open into a silent 'Oh' of delight as she was greeted by three magnificent oils.

John Tamerton, when he hadn't been painting the seemingly obligatory biblical scenes so beloved of the Victorians, had enjoyed painting village children. They were children of rosy cheeks and chubby form, yet from obviously poor backgrounds, sometimes accompanied by maidens in little cotton pinafores and bonnets, or in front of cottages; in other words he had enjoyed painting what were known as rustic subjects.

None of them was a work that Sue knew, but one in particular caught and held her attention. It portrayed a young girl standing outside a picturesque cottage. Around her feet were four or five geese, and in her hand she carried a slender wand. Her fair hair fell in a tumbling mass beneath her cotton cap, and for all her poor clothes Sue knew this was a picture of her grandmother.

'It's quite extraordinary that there should still be such a strong family resemblance after all this time. If John Tamerton were to walk in on us now he'd definitely recognise you.' The overtone of amusement in Edwin Ashley's voice couldn't hide the fact that he was very much aware of her, and that put her back on the defensive.

'You know, then? You know that's my grandmother?'

'Certainly I do.' He gave her his lazy smile. 'There is another portrait, a head and shoulders, that is held by the National Collections and is on show among other West Country artists in Exeter. But of course the most famous portrait of them all, the *Goat Girl*, is known to us only by engravings. By repute that was supposed to be your grandmother's own personal bequest when the old man died, but the painting hasn't been seen since his death, has it?' Edwin Ashley finished this little speech on an upward, querying note, but Sue had now recovered her equilibrium and was ready for him. Her face, turned towards him, held nothing but the most innocent of interested expressions.

'Goodness, you have done your homework!' she told him, not troubling to hide her admiration. 'But I have to confess that I'm surprised... I mean, John Tamerton was a good artist but he wasn't that brilliant. He can't be compared to the real "greats" of his time, can he?'

'Maybe not, but I think you're underrating him a little. There is considerable interest abroad in his work.'

'Abroad?' she queried.

'Yes. The Japanese are extremely fond of Victorian art at the moment. In fact it's my acting on instructions from one particular gallery in Tokyo that has meant you have been so unlucky just recently. They seem to have a particular—er—yen, shall we say, for John Tamerton's work?'

Sue rewarded his gentle pun with a grin, but as he smiled back at her, allowing his eyes to soften under shared amusement, she was aware for the first time of a quickening of her heartbeats that spelled danger. It would be very easy indeed to fall under this man's spell, but she couldn't help feeling suspicious that for the moment anyway her main interest to him was because she was the artist's great-granddaughter.

'I suppose these pictures are for sale?'

'I'm afraid not.' The smile slowly died on his face. 'They're on loan. I'm a planning a John Tamerton retrospective. I don't suppose you have anything you'd care to lend me for a couple of months?'

Sue looked back at him, considering. She really wanted to copy that small oil of her grandmother painted outside the family cottage in Sussex. John Tamerton had had his main studio in Hampstead but he'd also owned the pretty little country cottage which had been the basis of so many of his rural scenes. It had been a blow to have missed that last watercolour just because it had featured the cottage, but maybe, if Edwin Ashley would agree, she could make a copy of this picture instead.

'I might, if you'll let me copy that portrait!'

She was pleased to see that he looked utterly disconcerted. 'You paint?'

'Yes, I do. No, I haven't inherited his talent, but I am able to copy things rather well. In fact that's how I earn my living...'

'Good heavens!' He still looked as if he didn't quite believe her.

'Why are you so surprised? It's not that odd a career, is it? I assure you I'm quite well-known, and no, I don't do fakes, although I've been approached a number of times!' She smiled at him. 'By quite surprising people as well; people one would have thought would know better!'

He appeared to have pulled himself together. 'I imagine that's a tribute to your work!' he answered smoothly. 'Would I be wrong in thinking you specialise in Victorian art?'

'No, you'd be quite correct. Well, is it a deal? I'll lend you my six watercolours, if you'll let me copy my grandmother and the geese?'

It was impossible to mistake how keenly interested she was in the picture. That had been obvious from the first moment she'd seen it. Was it because she recognised so much of herself in it? Edwin Ashley shook his head; she hadn't even bothered to walk through to the next room, which held a number of John Tamerton's watercolours.

'As that particular picture belongs to me, OK, you've got a deal!' He watched her expressive eyes light up. 'But——' he held up one finger '—you'll have to do it on my terms. She doesn't leave the gallery. I

have a studio at the back. You'll have to work there.'
He saw the disappointment in her face.

'But that won't be possible. I have to work at home!'

Edwin shrugged. 'I'm sorry, but I can't let it go. It's insured on the clear understanding that it remains on the premises of the Ashley Gallery.'

'Couldn't you change the insurance?' she pleaded.

'Why should I? If you really want to to make a copy, you'll find a way.'

Sue looked at him resentfully. He was quite right, of course, but she didn't want to spend time here. He was too unsettling, and Georgina Foliot—well, both of them had looked at each other and disliked what they'd seen. She gave a big sigh because she knew she was going to be forced to capitulate.

'May I take photographs? If you'll allow me to do that I will be able to do a considerable amount of preliminary work at my own studio.'

'I already have some pretty detailed photographs of my own which I could lend you...'

'Have you?' she interjected in a hurry. 'That would be great. I can work quite well from photographs if they're sufficiently detailed because of course I know so well how John Tamerton painted.'

'So, you've copied his work before?'

Sue could have bitten her tongue out with frustration at allowing herself to be caught out by such a simple question as that, so there was a slight check before she answered.

'Why, yes, yes, I have. Someone I know locally has one of his pictures and I was lucky enough to get permission to copy it a couple of years ago.'

'What was it, a rustic or biblical scene?'

'Rustic.' Feeling uncomfortable, she began to walk towards the other room which had a number of watercolours hanging on the walls. They weren't all Tamertons by any means, but there were enough to distract her for a short time. She jumped slightly as she heard his voice, uncomfortably close behind her.

'By the way, there's a small Tamerton oil that's coming up at Christie's in South Kensington next week. It isn't of any interest to me, but would you like me to try and get it for you? You dropped out at just under a thousand, didn't you?'

'An oil? Why isn't it of interest to you? Is it damaged or something?'

'No, no, nothing like that. It's just that the subject in the picture is looking down, and the Japanese won't buy any painting where the eyes aren't turned upwards.'

'Really?' She wasn't sure if he was teasing her.

'It's perfectly true, I promise you. You can ring up Christie's, or Sotheby's for that matter, to check if you like.'

'How extraordinary!'

'I suppose it does sound a little weird, but I can assure you it's a fact.'

'Well, in that case, why not, always supposing it is—er—a good painting?'

'I think it's rather charming, so there may be a bit of competition, but I'll do my best.'

'Thank you very much... Look, I've got to be going; I'm driving home today, and that's a good four-hour drive.'

'Before you dash off come up to the office and give me your address and phone number. I've got the photographs there of my little goose girl, so you can take them with you if they're any good.' She wondered at the possessive affection she heard in his voice. Did his awareness of her have anything to do with her likeness to her grandmother?

'Do you come up to London often?' he continued.

'It all depends on the work. Sometimes I have to spend time here, but I prefer to be in the country.'

'That's unusual for a girl with your looks. I'd have thought you'd be more interested in making it in London; having a good time...' There was just the faintest hint of disparagement in his voice, as if he couldn't quite accept what she said, and the lids had dropped slightly over his eyes, giving him a definitely cynical look.

'I don't know how old you think I am, Mr Ashley——' she started off in a heated manner, but he interrupted,

'Edwin, please!'

'OK, Edwin! But I'm twenty-six years old and have slightly grown out of my disco years. When I was at art college it was parties every night, but I've calmed down since then, and am now able to go for weeks at a time without any withdrawal symptoms at all!'

He heard the sarcasm behind her words, and his brown eyes glinted down at her, but she couldn't read his expression.

'You don't look twenty-six; more like twenty-one!' That deep, sexy voice couldn't hide the faint disapproval she had sensed earlier, and as she couldn't think of a single reason why he should feel that way her temper rose.

'I don't carry my passport round with me for you to check, so you'll have to take my word for it; but I have to say it's usually older men who are so preoccupied with a girl's supposed youth!' He gave an unwilling laugh as he followed her up the stairs.

'I'm thirty-three next week. Want to come up for my birthday party?'

She looked back down at him over her shoulder.

'Would it be worth a four-hour drive?'

Just for a moment there was a silence between them, one charged with unspoken words, as his eyes locked with hers. She found herself strongly attracted to him, and didn't doubt for one minute that he felt the same way, although there was something about his expression that was unreadable. Maybe she'd better qualify that by saying he was interested in her possibly only as a descendent of John Tamerton? She was assailed by that strange weakness that left her feeling trembling and a little helpless. She was a fool to have responded to his casual words.

'I think that's something only you could answer, after the event!' he answered, slowly.

'Yes, well, I don't think I'll take the risk after all!' she responded.

'I would never have taken you for a coward!' he taunted as he followed her out on to the upper floor of the gallery, but she didn't respond as Georgina was already on her way over to them. She ignored Sue totally, concentrating on her boss.

'Booker rang. I think it's urgent, so I said you'd call back immediately?'

'OK. Can you get the photos of the girl with the geese for me? Miss Rivers is going to borrow them...' Sue managed to ignore the faintly raised eyebrows. 'Come into the office, Miss Rivers, or may I now call you Susan?'

'Make it Sue,' she smiled. 'That's what all my friends call me.' His response was disappointingly cool.

'Thank you. Now why don't you write down your address and phone number while you wait for the photos? I'll make my call, then we'll have that coffee I promised, unless you'd prefer tea?'

'I think I'll pass, if you'll forgive me.' Sue was writing down her address. 'I really must get home. What do I do about money if you're successful?'

'Don't worry, I'll be in touch. It's been a pleasure to meet you—er—Sue.' His voice had lowered a little over her name, and she couldn't help the pink in her cheeks becoming a little deeper. 'I hope I manage to get the Tamerton for you. Perhaps it'll help to make up for all those ones you lost.'

'Don't be silly! As you said, business is business...' She took refuge in bluntness. 'Anyway, as I said, I'm lucky to have my watercolours, and you owe me nothing!'

Georgina walked back in with a large manila envelope, and was obviously pleased that Sue was planning to leave so quickly.

'I'll be in touch...' Sue walked out, rather too quickly for good manners, turning her back almost with relief on one of the most attractive men she'd ever met in her life. She'd been secretly afraid of him living up to her expectations, ever since she'd caught her first glimpse of him at one of the sales.

CHAPTER TWO

SUE found it hard in the following days to keep her mind on her work. She discovered it was depressingly easy to allow a dark-eyed, dramatic-looking man to dominate her undisciplined thoughts. His really was the sort of face and figure that invited the unwary to weave dreams about. Not, she told herself firmly, that she intended to be one of those. No, she'd already learnt that painful lesson. Once before in her life she'd allowed her dreams to colour reality, and that had proved an extremely painful experience.

All the same, Edwin Ashley... Gosh, she thought, that's a marvellously romantic, Victorian name... Once more her imagination leapt ahead of reality until she firmly restrained herself. Even so she was forced to admit that just thinking about him had stirred up her heart, reminding her that that organ wasn't as dead as she'd once thought.

Maybe it was about time she started to look around again without those jaundiced feelings that damned all men just for quietly fancying her! At least it would make old Bridget happy. She'd never made any secret of the fact that she'd thoroughly disapproved of Sue's decision to base herself alone in her grandmother's cottage, in spite of the fact that it was the only home she could remember. Bridget had wanted her in London, where, in her own words, she'd 'meet people'.

There was no real denying, though, that she found him an attractive man, although she couldn't help wondering if her appeal for him was purely physical. She had a strong, if irrational feeling that maybe he had an ulterior motive in seeking her out so blatantly.

Today was the auction so she allowed her thoughts more latitude than usual, pondering on what he had told her about the Japanese only buying paintings if the subjects had their eyes raised. She thought too about her great-grandfather and how a modicum of her talent must have come direct from him, and how he had lived his life to the full. Yet one of her girlfriends, easily the most beautiful as well as the most talented, had told her long ago that she never intended to have such an intense relationship with any man that it could end in marriage. She saw that, and motherhood, as a trap, denying her her chance to fulfil her potential as an artist.

Yet Sue too thought of herself as an artist, but she'd never thought of denying herself the chance to become a mother just because of it. Perhaps that just meant she didn't have Ann's huge talent. She leant forward, her hands on her chin, deep in thought. A few years ago that thought would have depressed her, but now she felt a kind of release, a gratitude that she'd never have to take that kind of decision.

It proved at the start of the morning to be hard work to discipline herself sufficiently for her painting, but she was lucky enough, once she managed to sink herself into the work she was copying, to find this particular artist's brush strokes came easily to her. Once started she found it hard to break off, painting through lunch without a thought to hunger, totally engrossed in the view of the Thames above Westminster which was busily coming to life under her brush.

Her palette swirled under the build-up of colours, the soft smokiness of London's coal fires already committed by her to canvas; the great barges full of their murky wealth just waiting for their chance to blue the early autumn air further. It was a painting so evocative of its time, the scenery so much the same, yet so different, that she found herself wishing that she too had been alive in that slower age.

The persistent ringing of the phone dragged her back to the present, making her aware for the first time that she was stiff-fingered and exhausted from her work. 'Coming, I'm coming,' she called out impatiently, wiping her hands on a heavily turpentined rag.

'Yes?' She tucked the receiver under her chin to free her hands for further cleansing.

'Sue? Is that you?' Edwin's voice had her firmly standing to attention, the rag dropped on to the floor.

'Hi! Yes, it's me,' she replied ungrammatically.

'I thought you'd like to know...' his voice sounded so deep, so sexy that she found herself half smiling at her reflection in the nearby mirror '...that I managed to pick up the Tamerton today for nine hundred and fifty, including commission and tax.'

'You didn't!' she exclaimed, half disbelieving but wanting to be delighted.

'I did. Of course it's a small picture, as you'd expect from the price, but I hope you're pleased?'

'How can you ask? Thank you so much, Edwin. I must say I'm longing to see it.'

'I suppose you want to make quite sure you haven't been sold a pup! If you don't like it, you won't have to have it, you know. I'll be able to find another buyer quite easily, so you needn't feel pressured.'

'I'm sure I shall love it, but I'm not sure when I shall be able to come up and collect it. Will you keep it for me?'

'Of course, but as I'm expected in the West Country to value some paintings for a client tomorrow, how about me acting as delivery man and later on giving you dinner?'

After that conversation it was impossible for Sue to settle to any more work. Happily she cleaned her brushes as she allowed her inner excitement to mount, before a nasty inner voice began to pour cold water on her thoughts. Was Edwin as keen to meet her again as she was to see him? Or was it just John Tamerton's great-granddaughter he was coming to see?

Once she'd finished tidying away her work, she stood back and looked around her critically. If Edwin was going to call to see her tomorrow, then no doubt he would be interested to see her pictures. She hadn't as yet made a start on copying his portrait of the little goose girl, but then wouldn't he expect to see a copy by her of John Tamerton's work? She bit her lip. The large oil facing her would definitely have to be hidden from him, so she would have to find something to take its place. The trouble was, what?

'Well! If I'd known that I'd have to go into the home removal business just to satisfy your ideas of what the studio should look like for your latest boyfriend, I'd have stayed at home!'

Sue swung round to look at Bridget, her eyes full of laughter.

'I thought you'd be pleased a man was coming to see me here!' she answered provocatively.

'That's as may be!' Bridget shook her head grimly. 'But you know I don't think it's right, a young girl living here all alone!'

Sue grinned. 'I'll be fine here, and you know it! Why, I've lived here most of my life after all.'

Bridget shook out a duster vigorously. 'I hope you're satisfied, and if you're not, don't expect me to do any more moving of pictures! Anyway, you didn't live here all alone, and I know it's not what your Gran wanted for you.' She gave an eloquent sniff.

'Thanks, Bridget. I'm really grateful...' Sue gave her a hug, but it seemed she wasn't to be mollified.

'I can't imagine why you want to hide your copy of the Tamerton picture of your grandmother with the nanny-goat and kid. It's beautiful in its own right.'

'You haven't seen the original!'

Bridget gave her a curious look. 'There's some secret attached to it, isn't there?'

'Not really a secret, let's just say family problems...'

'You know if that Edwin Ashley saw it he'd almost certainly want to put it in his show. So why do you want to hide it?'

Sue sank down on to a stool, her expression pensive. 'It's a long story; do you really want to hear it?'

'I'm all ears. Let me just fill up the kettle and make some tea, then we can sit out in the yard.' Sue followed her out, the late afternoon sun still slanting on to the stone buildings, the old cobbles warm underfoot. She sat down on the old wooden bench, not caring that it was dirty and covered with lichen. She looked around her, at the tiny farmhouse with the barn attached, the run-down shippens facing her. This had been her grandmother's home; also her father's after he'd lost all his money. It had a tiny orchard at the end of the yard, and an even smaller garden in the front, and faced on to a little-used lane just outside the village.

Unpretentious, it was also cosy and perhaps a little too picturesque. Not for the first time Sue wondered if her grandmother had chosen to live here because it reminded her of the cottage of her youth.

'Here...' Bridget handed her a mug. She raised her own mug to her mouth. 'Cheers, dear! Although, come to think of it, maybe we should drink to your grandma. I never cease to be full of gratitude that she left this place only to you and not to be shared with those French cousins of yours...'

Sue smiled, although her salutation was a silent one as she remembered the small but indomitable figure of her grandmother. 'Well, go on then, dear, I'm waiting.' Bridget's voice brought her back to the present.

'You know my grandmother left everything to me?'

'Yes, of course I do!' Bridget answered impatiently. 'Haven't I just said so?'

'But you don't know that my two cousins were more than a bit peeved that they got nothing.'

Bridget was silent for a moment, considering. 'I suppose that's understandable. After all, she was their grandmother as well.'

'They weren't really interested in this house. All they wanted were her pictures. She didn't have many of her father's works, just the four you've seen. I thought it was a bit unfair that they should have been left out so I asked Gran's solicitor if he thought I should give them one picture each——' She broke off, her brows drawn together in a frown.

'Don't tell me!' Bridget interrupted. 'He wouldn't let you, and the cousins were furious because you'd already told them what you'd hoped to do!'

Sue sighed. 'Yes... but it wasn't as easy as that. What they really wanted was the one picture that Gran had kept hidden all these years. The one that hasn't been seen in public since it left John Tamerton's studio when he died. I'd already promised Gran that when she died I'd keep it safe. After her death I left it hidden away where she kept it because that was what she wanted me to do. In fact I tried to deny all knowledge of it. Unfortunately Linda, one of my cousins, came here unexpectedly and saw my copy. She didn't believe me when I told her it was a copy. She thinks it's the original.'

Bridget shook her head in incomprehension. 'Why should your grandmother have wished to keep the picture hidden? It's had an engraving done of it, so why the secrecy?'

'I don't know, I wish I did... But if I let it come to light somehow, don't you see what will happen? The cousins will accuse me of cheating the Inland Revenue and I'll be forced to sell it because I won't be able to pay the duty on it, and everyone will think I was just being dishonest in keeping it hidden!'

'By the sound of it you were wrong to try to do anything for these cousins of yours!'

'Yes, that's what the solicitors told me afterwards, but it seemed so unfair...'

'You and your soft heart! Oh, well! What happened next?'

'They tried to have Gran's will overset. They said I'd used "undue influence" or something.'

'But she'd virtually brought you up!' Bridget answered, scandalised. 'I mean after your mother pushed off to the States and there was the divorce—well, of course she'd be specially fond of you.'

'Yes, well, they didn't see it that way. They thought my father had been given more than his share when his debts were paid. Anyway, they didn't go ahead with their threat, but it's been unpleasant.'

'If they didn't succeed what have you got to worry about now?'

'I've told you! If they find out about the picture, then I won't have a leg to stand on. They'll probably sue me and make sure I end up with nothing!'

Bridget blew out her cheeks as they both sat, silent, but it was Sue who broke the silence. 'I've got to try and find out what the mystery was, don't you agree? There had to be a good reason why Gran kept that work hidden all these years. I mean, she was a very old lady indeed when she finally died.'

'She was ninety-six years old!' Bridget replied with pride. 'And we all thought she'd make her century, but the lord thought otherwise...'

'That picture was painted in the closing years of the last century. It's also supposed to be one of John Tamerton's best, if not his last major work,' Sue mused. 'He did very little after that because his sight was failing, and that's extraordinary in itself, isn't it?

That he should have painted so wonderfully at the end of his career...'

'What are you trying to get at?' Bridget was puzzled.

'Do you think Gran hid that painting, and these others here, away because she knew John Tamerton hadn't painted them?'

Bridget looked at her, her brows drawn together in a frown, but unusually seemed to have nothing to say.

'Good God! Of course I'm right!' Sue exclaimed. 'Now why didn't I think of that before? There's only one person it could have been. Augustus Frome was a young boy from the village. John Tamerton taught him to paint, and let him work in his Sussex studio... What I can't understand,' she continued, 'is how no one has thought or suggested this before.' She was silent, thinking it out. Then,

'I suppose it's not so strange if you know the story. Augustus died before he had a chance to prove himself. It was a ghastly tragedy, I suppose, because he already had TB as a child, so his time must always have been limited. My guess is that these paintings Gran kept here were mainly his work, not her father's...'

'How old was she when Augustus died?' Bridget enquired.

'Well, she must have been about thirteen or fourteen when he—if it was him—painted her with the angora goats, and I don't think he lived very long after that.'

'Old enough to have had a crush on him, wouldn't you think?' Bridget gave a sly smile.

'I don't know... Yes, I suppose so...' Sue's mind was wandering in a different direction. 'I wonder why she didn't tell anybody?' It didn't take her long to work that one out. 'Loyalty to her father's reputation, I suppose. I mean, he must have claimed credit for that picture, mustn't he, because it's signed with his name?'

'You'd have thought she'd try to put the matter right after his death,' Bridget answered austerely, but Sue was still following her own thoughts.

'Good heavens! She's left the whole problem to me!'

Once Sue had admitted the idea that someone else could have been responsible for these paintings, she was amazed to look back and accept how many hints her grandmother had given her over the years. She must have found me very stupid! she told herself, recalling countless conversations when her grandmother had spoken of the past. Indeed, latterly, the past had become more important than the present, and it had been her grandmother's constant talk about her youth that initially had helped Sue become so interested in the Victorians and their art.

'Are you sure there wasn't a letter or something?' Bridget queried, her eyes quite bright with excitement.

'No, there was nothing. I think the only clue was the fact that she kept these pictures here and refused to loan them out, or let anyone, apart from the family, see them!'

'She must have suffered terrible guilt, particularly if she was fond of him; Augustus, I mean...' Bridget's expression was full of interest; romance in any form was still of prime interest in her life. 'Does anyone know what he looked like, or anything about him?'

Sue shook her head. 'Not as far as I know, although nobody's really done an in-depth study of John Tamerton. He wasn't one of the real greats of his time like Millais or Landseer. He was a member of the Royal Academy, and he had considerable popular acclaim in his life. Anyway, his work is now becoming fashionable again, and some of the larger pictures could be making big money!'

Bridget's eyes lit up once more with vicarious pleasure.

'So, you could be sitting on a fortune!' she breathed dramatically.

'His work, yes, but not pictures painted by a shadowy figure called Augustus Frome who died young!'

'Are your pictures here signed?'

'Funnily enough, no, they aren't, except the goat girl, of course.'

'I suppose John Tamerton realised he'd have to sign that if he were to claim it as his own.'

Sue had been thinking silently, only half her mind concentrating on their conversation.

'You know, I think Gran would have liked me to tell the world about Augustus Frome!'

Bridget laughed at her. 'That's my girl! Always the champion of the underdog!' But she suddenly became more serious. 'Anyway, I happen to agree with you over this. If the poor chap died so young I think the world is entitled to know just what it missed, don't you?'

Sue's eyes were sparkling with inner enthusiasm. 'You're right! And I think I know just the way it can be done!' But she refused to tell Bridget how she thought this might be accomplished.

Sue was pleased that Bridget wasn't going to be around when Edwin called. She didn't trust the older woman's belief that all men were potential husbands for her, and she was still more than a little unsure of Edwin's reasons for coming down to Devon to see her. All the same, while she was up in her room, still deciding on the finishing touches of a supposedly completely casual outfit, she heard a car draw up outside.

Deciding that to spray herself with her favourite scent would be too much of a come-on at this stage, she peered out of her window, taking care not to be seen from outside.

A large and rather beautiful classic old car was parked outside the cottage, its gleaming coachwork of dark green somehow not blending in at all with nature's exuberant shades of the same colour. It was difficult to take in all its glory from her present angle, so she decided that her unusual shyness had to be overcome fast. No doubt she'd get plenty of opportunity to see the car at closer quarters later.

She ran lightly down the stairs, the intricate maze of patterns on her leggings drawing the eyes to her legs. Her large loose-knitted cotton top in plain white ended in a crocheted fringe and was in a healthy contrast to the glow of health on her face, and if her colour was a bit high, well, she had an excuse, didn't she? She was excited at being able to see for the first time the picture Edwin was bringing down from London.

'Hi! You found me, then?'

He gave her a long, lazy smile, taking his time before answering, and her blood-pressure shot up while she waited expectantly. What a pity... but she broke that thought off in a hurry.

'Yes, your directions were pretty good, although I don't think the Devon lanes were quite made for my car!'

'What is it?' Her curiosity had overcome her good manners, and, afraid he'd realise she'd peeped from her window, she walked into the kitchen to collect a bottle of wine in one hand, and two glasses in the other.

'It's a Bentley. A real old classic from the thirties...'

'That's clever of you to have found one! I mean, normally they sell for an absolute——' She broke off, embarrassed.

He smiled, and continued. 'A fortune? Yes, you're right, although I have to say I inherited mine.'

Edwin's easy manners helped them through the first slight awkwardness between them, although she had to admit that the talk about cars, three and a half litres, original Vanden Plas tourers, passed her by as she studied this man who seemed so intent on entering her life.

She noticed that although he was talking politely enough to her his eyes were searching the walls, studying the pictures hanging there, then he suddenly smiled straight at her.

'You're containing your impatience very well!'

Just for a moment she looked back at him, her expression non-committal in the extreme, until his slightly raised eyebrows brought her smartly to her senses. Her colour deepened again as she looked away a little awkwardly, almost as if he had caught her out in some dubious practice.

'I'm sorry, I was wool-gathering...'

'So I gathered. Where were you, if it's not a rude question? Or is it no good asking because you keep your thoughts and dreams firmly to yourself?'

Deciding that she didn't quite like the way the conversation was turning out, Sue walked over to join him in front of the small window.

'Well, where is it?' she demanded, her eyes full of an expression that wasn't too easy to read.

'Right here!' his eyes teased, as he held up a briefcase.

'Goodness, it really is small!'

'Yes, I think he must have done it originally as a study of a child's head for one of his larger pictures, don't you?'

Sue took the small picture from him and held it in her hands. The ornate gilded frame didn't quite manage to overshadow the apple-cheeked urchin whose personality was always going to overcome his surroundings. The picture of bucolic innocence, he perhaps lacked the superficial charm of prettier children, but he was so obviously about to be up to mischief that her mouth tilted in a smile of pleasure.

'Oh, yes! It's charming.'

'You really like him?' he queried.

'Most certainly!' she agreed emphatically, her eyes narrowed critically, as she studied the work before her with a professional eye.

'He knew his stuff, John Tamerton. Look at those skin tones! I should say you've certainly got a bargain.' Edwin's admiration was open and quite unfeigned, and Sue, giving him a quick look, realised he was being completely honest.

'Yes...' Edwin had moved uncomfortably close to study the little painting. 'As an artist he has been considerably underrated in my opinion. Look at the freedom in those brush strokes, yet it is always a controlled freedom.'

Sue tried to remain impervious to his closeness, but, finding herself uncomfortable, moved away.

'Anyone who is lucky enough to own this small person should hang him in their bedroom facing the bed so that when they wake up each morning they should be reminded of their own childhood.'

Edwin silently laughed at her, as if he too would like to start his day opposite her, a wicked gleam in his eyes that spoke more eloquently than any words. Wow, she thought, perhaps he *is* really interested in me after all!

'Now you've got that major point settled, how about showing me your own collection of John Tamerton's work?'

She gave him one of her clear-eyed glances. 'By all means. Would you like a drink before we start?' Sue gestured towards the bottle she'd carried in.

'I'd rather wait if you don't mind. By the way, is there anywhere I can park my car off the road? It's too wide for comfort for this part of the world, I know, and I'd rather not have someone discover that fact the painful way.'

'Yes, there's a drive a little further on that will bring you round the back into the yard.'

'Thanks. I shouldn't really be driving it at all because its almost a museum piece, but it was the pride and joy of my old uncle Ben and I haven't the heart to get rid of it because he loved it so much.'

'What on earth do you do with it in London?' Sue asked.

'I keep it in the garage mostly; it only comes out for long country runs, when I have to do a trip like this one, for instance. All my friends tell me it is indeed worth a fortune and I ought to sell it, but I feel the old boy would turn in his grave if I did any such thing!'

'I've never seen the point of owning anything unless you can enjoy it,' Sue said. 'I spend half my time copying pictures that the owners can't afford to insure to hang on their walls. The original is locked away in some safety-deposit box somewhere, and they hang my copy in pride of place instead!'

'Yes, that's become quite a problem, hasn't it? I suppose it's because everything seems to have been caught in a vicious spiral of rising prices. A few years ago you would have been able to buy one of your great-grandfather's watercolours for about a hundred pounds; today you will have to pay anything between one and three thousand pounds!'

'Yes, I can never quite understand why... I mean, is there more money around?'

'Not necessarily, although I think it is spread a little wider than it used to be. No, I think the great majority of people now have pleasure in owning things from the past. There seems to be a pretty good chance too that things go up in value, and if they can be ahead of trends then they can make money as well as enjoy living with their investment.'

'Neatly put! And no doubt good for a business like yours.' Sue couldn't resist that last sly little dig.

'These things are cyclical,' he responded. 'There are good years and there are bad years. That's what one has to remember—that the good times don't last forever. Now, if you'll excuse me, I'll go and move my car.'

Sue was left looking at the unused bottle and glasses with wry amusement. Well, for the second time she'd been given the indication that he could be interested in her. All the same, she thought, I'm not too sure I want to lose my heart to him. She hadn't been able to help noticing that he was having a jolly good check on the pictures, and that definitely showed he had an ulterior motive in seeking her out, didn't it?

It was a good thing she'd put a guard on her heart because she didn't think it would do her much good to fall in love with him. He wasn't here today because he found her irresistible, oh, no! Mind you, there was nothing intrinsically wrong in combining business with pleasure, just as long as she stayed aware of what the real motivation had to be.

Sue's eyes suddenly danced. She'd got her own plans in that department. He needn't think he's the only one to take advantage of an opportunity, she thought.

She was going to be Augustus Frome's new champion, and she was prepared for a fight! Something told her that he might not be too pleased to hear that she was planning to chip a few dents into John Tamerton's reputation.

Something also told her that it was a good thing that she held a trump card, and that she'd better go out and join him, because she didn't think he was going to be happy until he'd seen into nearly every room in the house!

No more disappearing into a dream, Sue, she told herself firmly. You're going to need all your wits about you if you're not going to be taken for a ride! Now you'd better be on your way. My guess is that he will already be in the studio!

She walked out over the cobbled yard, deliberately making no secret that she was on her way to join him. Mr Ashley might think that everything was going very nicely his way, but she'd soon show him that he was mistaken. It was a pity about the picture of that jolly-looking small urchin, but she wasn't open to bribes, and it would be better if he understood that fact right from the start of their acquaintance.

'You don't mind? I couldn't resist the chance to look at your work!' Sue walked over to join him. He was standing critically in front of her latest work. 'This is very good indeed...'

'Yes, I find that particular artist quite easy to copy, but of course that isn't always the case.'

'I can imagine. Do you turn work down?'

'Yes, I often have to, I'm afraid, but latterly people seem to have realised that I specialise in nineteenth-century work, which makes my life easier.'

'I'd love to see your Tamerton copies.'

'You've already seen two of them.' He looked startled.

'You mean those two watercolours in your sitting-room are your work?' She gave him her dancing smile and nodded. His brown eyes had narrowed and he looked a bit shaken.

'You could have fooled me. I thought they were originals.'

Again she smiled. 'You didn't study them very closely. If you looked again I think you'd know... Anyway, you needn't worry. I don't churn them out, you know, and I always sign them with my own name.'

'I thought you worked in oils?'

'I do, mostly. I only use watercolours for my own work, or to copy John Tamerton's. My grandmother liked to see me to do it; she told me I'd learn to paint better that way.'

'Ah, yes, your grandmother... I suppose you don't by any chance know what has happened to that rather famous picture that John Tamerton painted of her when she was a child?'

Sue looked back at him, her face for once completely serious. 'That's why you came to see me here, isn't it? The picture, that was just a sweetener, wasn't it, to give you a chance to look around?'

His rather heavy black brows drew together in a frown. 'I think that's rather over-simplifying my motives——' he began, but she interrupted,

'Don't try to patronise me, Edwin Ashley! It might suit you to think that I'm just a country bumpkin at heart, and one that doesn't know her way around the salerooms, but you'd be wrong!' She gave him a cynical smile. 'I rang Christie's to check just how much that Tamerton oil had gone for. You got your sums a bit wrong, didn't you? They told me it went under the hammer at two thousand two hundred pounds!'

CHAPTER THREE

EDWIN'S skin became suffused with a dull red as he stood looking at her.

'I wish you hadn't done that——' he started to say, but Sue interrupted.

'I bet you do!' So sure was she of her ground that she allowed him to see a little of her contempt. That turned out to be a mistake.

'You really think you're clever.' His mouth twisted a little with disgust. 'It's a pity you've made up your mind why I should have chosen to let you have that picture, because you couldn't be further from the truth!' There was a look on his face that forced her to try once more to defend her position.

'Prove it!' she spat at him, defiance obvious in every line of her body. He visibly relaxed as he allowed his eyes to wander over her, their insolent appraisal raising the temperature between them almost to boiling-point.

'I don't suppose anybody could do that to your total satisfaction,' he drawled, 'but if you checked with the auctioneer who actually handled that sale you would find out that he knew I was bidding for that picture on your behalf. He happens to be a friend of mine and was interested to hear about your connection with John Tamerton. He knew that if it went over your limit I intended, within reason, to try to ensure it came to you.' He stopped for a moment, his narrowed eyes watching carefully the expression on her face.

'I never had any intention of bribing you, and I can't imagine why you should think I would want to.' He looked the question, one eyebrow slightly raised, but as she remained silent he continued. 'Anyway, you got that picture because I felt sorry for you; because I'd consistently outbid you at the last half a dozen sales. Once I found out who you were I felt a little guilty because all the pictures I'd bought were destined to go abroad. I've made a handsome profit already out of John Tamerton. It seemed right that I should try to redress the balance a little for his great-granddaughter.'

He saw the slightly shattered expression on her face, and his lips split in a sarcastic smile. 'I suppose you want me to leave?'

'No! Don't go.' She had stretched out a hand, as if to detain him, then he gave her a charming smile.

'Am I forgiven so easily, then?' The smile became teasing. 'Now that I do find surprising. I quite expected to be given my marching orders, particularly as you've made it more than clear that you're immune to my obviously less than fatal charms. Anyway, you don't exactly strike me as someone who finds it easy to admit she's made a mistake.'

Now these guileless comments really put poor Sue in a quandary. If he had been telling the truth, and, goodness, she really wanted to believe that he had, then there would be nothing easier than to smile and apologise gracefully. On the other hand, suppose it was just a clever bit of spur-of-the-moment manipulation?

Either way she had to make up her mind quickly, and it didn't take her long to do so. She needed this man at the moment, so there was little point in antagonising him. She gracefully shrugged her shoulders.

'I'm sorry if I've misjudged you, but if you're honest admit that I had, on the surface, good cause.'

'Well, yes, I suppose so, but I'm still intrigued trying to guess what possible good you think could come to me from trying to put you in my debt. You don't really think I'm the sort of man who has to blackmail women to get their attention, do you? I quite understand that you don't appear to find me attractive, but even so I've never yet been driven to quite the lengths you seem to suggest could be necessary.' The wicked gleam in his eyes should have warned her that it could be dangerous to cross swords with him, but she didn't hesitate to accept the challenge.

'It would do you good to accept that you're not necessarily God's gift to every woman!' she smouldered in return, caution being cast to the winds. Dancing brown eyes were narrowed in amusement.

'I do! Particularly as far as grey-eyed blonds are concerned.' But Sue was too busy preparing to drop her own bombshell to really take in his teasing words.

'Anyway, I'm surprised you haven't worked it out for yourself. Of course, if you weren't so vain I expect you might have been slightly quicker on the uptake...' She stopped, furious, as he broke into laughter.

'You know, you're quite enchanting when you're angry...' Before she could stop him, he'd pulled her close to his body, and those teasing lips had stolen what should have been a fleeting kiss. Indeed it should have been nothing but the teasing gesture of a man determined to make her admit the physical attraction of their bodies, but his lips met hers with all the power of colliding atoms, provoking a reaction so severe and unexpected that it appeared to rock both of them off whatever pre-determined course they thought the stars had set for them. For one long moment they clung to each other, Sue greedily drinking in the electric sensations that chased over her body at the intimate proximity of his, until reality, inspired by the sudden tensing of his muscles, pulled her unwillingly back from his seductive touch. Furious with herself, as well as him, and this time determined to wipe the smile off his face, she blurted out what she believed to be the truth.

'You want to create a sensation with your retrospective by showing in public for the first time since the last century the picture of my grandmother with the angora goats!' The sudden quick blaze of excited light in the light brown eyes perversely made her heart sink like a stone. Now she knew exactly why he had bothered to come to see her. Oh! He could try to wrap it up in pretty speeches, but underneath it all the truth had stood out like a beacon. That kiss of his had just been the first attack on her defences, and perversely her response had horrified her. This man fought dirty!

'You know where it is? Everyone thought that it must have been destroyed, because after all what reason could your grandmother have had to keep it hidden all these years? I hoped you'd be able to tell me the story of what happened to it...' It was impossible for him to hide his excitement. Oh, the shame of her response to his treacherous touch! But at least it ensured that she managed to continue their conversation without him being too aware of the turmoil he'd created inside her. She knew, with a sickening feeling, that he was far too experienced a man not to have noted her response to his kiss, but desperately she refused to accept that knowledge.

'Yes, I know where it is, and what's more important why my grandmother kept it hidden all these years...' His brows drew together in a puzzled frown. 'Come and look at these...'

He drew in his breath sharply as she lifted an unframed picture that was one of a pile stacked against the wall and put it on to an easel. It showed a group of young children playing outside a group of cottages on the rough stony road. Without giving him time for any but the most superficial appreciation, she replaced each picture with another, until he'd seen all four.

'Well?' she queried. 'What do you think?'

'I think your grandmother was a very clever lady. She certainly picked what looks like some of the cream of her father's work, if these are anything to go by.'

Sue gave him a rigid little smile.

'I'm pleased you like them, but now brace yourself for a shock. They aren't the work of John Tamerton, and nor is the big picture of Gran. That's why she kept them hidden all these years. She knew who the real artist was, you see.'

The brown eyes narrowed as he scanned her face, then he turned away to look once more at the last picture she'd left on the easel.

'If you look carefully you'll see none of them is signed...'

He spun round quickly to look at her.

'The picture of the girl and the goats was signed by John Tamerton!'

She gave him a steady look.

'Yes, it was. That was why my grandmother took it and kept it hidden all these years. She wasn't strong enough herself to betray her father, and I think she left that job to me.'

'Who was the supposed artist?' he demanded, hardly bothering to hide the touch of sarcasm in his voice.

'Augustus Frome...'

'I've never heard of him!' Edwin replied scornfully.

'No, you wouldn't have, because I think these are all his works extant. He died before he had a chance to make a name for himself. He was John Tamerton's pupil; a local boy from the village. I think he might have been the son of the vicar, but I don't really know; I don't think anyone does...'

'Are you trying to tell me that a boy from the village grew up capable of doing that painting?'

'Hardly a village child if he was the vicar's son!' Sue snapped back. 'Anyway, I know very little about him, except that I think he painted these pictures, and it's about time he came out from under the shadow of John Tamerton and was recognised in his own right!'

Edwin Ashley stood looking at her, a frown on his face. The silence between them deepened, but it was he who broke it.

'You realise that if this gets about it could damage John Tamerton's reputation quite badly? That if there is a question that he didn't paint all his own pictures people might not be so keen to collect his work?'

'But there isn't any question of that, is there? It's just these five pictures! That's why my grandmother kept them all here.'

'Did she tell you in so many words that Augustus Frome painted these pictures?'

Sue was silent for a moment, honesty compelling her to tell the truth.

'Not exactly, no... But she did so by implication all the time. Latterly she talked a great deal about Augustus Frome, and why should she have done that if he wasn't important to her in some way?'

'So, this is really something you've decided for yourself?'

Sue bristled. 'You could say so... But it shouldn't be difficult to find an expert to confirm that these pictures were painted by someone other than John Tamerton!'

'Look, you must know that quite a number of successful artists employed pupils to help them with major works. They worked under the close supervision of the artist, and yet there has never been any question of acknowledging their contributions. Why are you so sure this wasn't the case here?'

'Because none of these pictures is signed. I think they were painted by the same hand as the goat girl. When you see it, you'll know what I mean!'

'You have it here?' It was impossible to hide Edwin Ashley's shock.

'Where else? Gran had a special hiding place made for it. Even I didn't know it existed until after my father died. She let me make a copy of it. That's when I heard so many of her stories about Augustus Frome. She used to sit with me while I worked and tell me stories about her childhood...' She looked up at him then, her expression fierce. 'Why would it be so wrong to tell the world about Augustus Frome? I'm sure that's what she wanted me to do!'

'Will you show me the picture?'

Sue bit her lip, indecision written in every line of her body.

'I don't want to show it to anybody until I know you're prepared to take this idea of mine seriously!' she said. 'If you want to show the picture of Gran, well, I'll think about it, as long as you also show these unsigned pictures which I think ought to be credited to Augustus Frome.'

'Have you discussed this with anyone else?'

'No. No, I haven't... I promised Gran, you see, that I'd never sell the pictures. That's why she left them to me and not to my cousins. She knew they'd get rid of them to the highest bidder...' He noted her fierce scorn for her cousin's behaviour.

She slid her eyes sideways from him, knowing she'd have to trust him, but she was still slightly afraid of letting him share all her secrets.

'It wasn't declared to the Inland Revenue. I'm afraid if I let it be seen now I'll have to pay tax on it, and I don't think I'll have enough money to do so.'

'Surely that's easily overcome!' he answered impatiently. 'You didn't find it until after her death.'

'One of my cousins came here after Gran died. She saw my painting and thought it was the original at first. When they found out it was only a copy they were furious. They've tried to make trouble already, but so far they haven't succeeded.'

'You have got yourself into a mess, haven't you?' His voice sounded light and a little hard.

'What would you have done?' Her voice did little to disguise her passionate feelings. 'She was my grandmother! The only person who really, truly loved me and cared what happened to me. Was I supposed to have broken her trust the minute she'd died? Let everyone see what she'd kept so carefully hidden all those years?'

'Calm down! There's no need to get so excited.'

She dashed an angry hand over her eyes. 'I'm sorry. I shouldn't have bothered you with this problem. Why don't you go away and forget it?'

'You must know that that's the very last thing I'll do! Look, you've come to me for help. For the moment perhaps we don't agree quite what that help should be, but surely that's something, with goodwill, that can be sorted out?'

'I suppose I have said too much to back down now,' she agreed, albeit a little shakily.

'You most certainly have. Now there are two things I want you to agree to. First, if you won't show me the original just yet, please can I see your copy? And secondly, I hope you're going to agree to come out and have dinner with me this evening, because we have a great deal to talk about, don't we?'

Sue wasn't proof against his smile, which made the brown eyes appear suddenly warm and understanding of her dilemma, even if she was far too aware of the danger in agreeing.

'OK... It's over there, under that dustsheet. I normally have it on the wall, but I thought with you coming here perhaps it would be better to keep it hidden. It isn't full-size or anything like it.' He helped her to prop it up, then stood back to look at it. Sue joined him, her eyes critical as she tried to judge it as impartially as he most certainly would.

She saw a younger version of herself, but one dressed in strange clothes, her shoulder-length hair mainly covered in a coarse linen bonnet that tied under her chin. Her dress was dark brown wool covered by a torn pinafore made of the same coarse linen as the bonnet. Her legs and feet were bare, just covered up to the ankles by clumsy-looking laced-up boots. The goats, one angora nanny and her kid, were painted in tremendous detail, as was the surrounding foliage of ivy, bracken and marguerites in the long grass.

The girl had her long, curving eyelids and a full, sensitive mouth. It was a pretty and appealing face, full of a delicate languor, and to the discerning eye there was something faintly erotic about the girl's close proximity to the goats—the nanny, so precisely painted, with her kid, his young horns giving him an undisputedly devilish air.

'My God, you're clever! But it's made me want to see the original more than ever.'

'Not yet! We've still got some problems to sort out, haven't we?'

'Hmm?' Edwin appeared to be miles away for a moment. 'Yes, I suppose we have... Now what about shutting everything up and coming out to dinner?'

'OK, but don't think you can walk all over me, because I have a mind of my own!'

'And you can say that again!' he agreed, *sotto voce*, as they both prepared to leave the studio.

* * *

As they sat over coffee in the restaurant they were both still aware that all their differences hadn't been overcome. Edwin at least seemed to have realised that for the moment business took precedence over pleasure as far as Sue was concerned.

'I still think it's a good idea to get someone who really knows John Tamerton's work well to study a couple of Gran's pictures. There must be someone who's considered an expert on his work...' she said.

'Yes, there is, but I'm not sure you'll be prepared to accept his judgement!'

'Why on earth not?' She tried to give him a rather haughty look. 'I'm just as open to reasonable opinions as anyone else, you know.'

'Ah! But you might not care for the expert.'

'Look, I know it suits you to think I'm prejudiced, but I'm not! Anyway, who is this man?'

'It's me!' There was a nasty silence.

'You?'

'I'm afraid so. I did warn you that you might find it difficult to accept this particular expert's judgement.' His amused expression at the conflict so revealingly displayed on her face emphasised cruelly her dilemma.

'B-but there must be somebody else surely?' she stuttered.

'Of course there is. Either Christie's or Sotheby's have experts in Victorian art who'd be delighted to help, but if there were any difficulty, any question of provenance, I have to warn you right now that they'd come to me! You see, I've written a couple of books about the less well-known artists working at the same time as John Tamerton. That particular time, the latter half of the nineteenth century, is my speciality.'

'I should have done my homework better!' Sue moaned. 'You must have been laughing at me!'

'No, not laughing at all. But I will tell you something. You should be able to tell yourself whether more than one hand has been employed in painting those pictures of your grandmother's. What I want to know is why you haven't done so.'

'I'm no expert,' she blustered, trying for time.

'I think you are. Certainly on Tamerton. So why?'

She gave him a fulminating glance between lowered lashes, but he sat there, as serene and calm as if what he was asking were of no particular importance at all. She found herself looking at his hands. These weren't the hands of a dilettante. They were long and slender-fingered, yes, and the nails well cared-for, but there was also an impression of strength, of someone able to handle all that life could throw at him. Slightly tanned, they played idly with the silver salt-cellar in front of him, the starched white linen of the cloth a perfect foil for their capable beauty.

'Because I haven't had time to really study the paintings. I have to work, you know!' she finished on a belligerent note.

'Now why do I get the feeling that you're trying to hide something?' He smiled down at her, one dark eyebrow raised in a question. At once she lowered her eyes.

'I can't imagine, but, if you must know, this is an idea I've been playing around with in my mind for some time. It isn't something that I've found particularly easy to accept either!'

'I see. So in spite of all that championing of Augustus Frome, you've held back from trying to prove anything one way or another.'

'I told you, I'm no *expert*.' Her scorn underlined the word. 'Nobody would believe anything I had to say! In fact if I tried on anything like that I'd probably end up with my cousins down on me like the proverbial ton of bricks, in case I upset their future plans for selling off their Tamertons!'

'Really? I didn't know they owned that many...'

'They probably don't now! That's why Gran was so keen to leave everything to me. She knew they were in the habit of selling one or two pictures every year. They have very expensive lifestyles, my cousins.'

'So you don't get on?'

Sue shrugged. 'No, not really, we never have. They've been brought up mainly in France. My aunt's French, you know, and of course they didn't approve of Daddy at all.'

'That sometimes happens in families—that brothers or sisters don't get on.' He flicked her a quick look which might have been compassion.

'Yes, well, you needn't feel sorry for me! Gran and I managed very well together, after all, and she was very fond of my father and enjoyed having him around.'

'I'm not! And you needn't sound quite so fierce. I'm not one of your cousins!'

Sue was becoming impatient. The dinner might have been delicious, but she'd hardly tasted any of it, being too taken up with the battle that had been going on between them all evening.

'Right. Are you going to study those pictures of mine? I really want to know if you think there's any chance they might have been painted by someone else.'

'You've made up your mind you want me to do the job?'

Once more she shrugged her shoulders. 'It doesn't seem as if I have much choice, does it?'

'That's a really gracious invitation. Now why would I get the impression that I'm definitely just about the last person you want to become involved with?' Sue tightened her lips at the smooth sarcasm, yet was there a quality of hurt under it? All the same, honesty compelled her to admit that she couldn't really blame him. Her manner had left a great deal to be desired when she'd asked him. She looked into his face and what she saw there caused her to rush into speech.

'You're going to refuse?' Just for a moment then she was swept by a feeling of such panic that she accepted she'd made what could turn out to be a drastic mistake. It was hard to hide her relief when she heard his next words.

'No, rather like you I have to agree that in these circumstances I too don't have much choice! Not least if we're ever to let the world admire what I think is going to be John Tamerton's final work!'

'And what will you do if it turns out to be painted by Augustus Frome?' Her voice was once more deceptively sweet, but Edwin noticed the stubborn line of her full lower lip. He gave her a long stare, then his eyes crinkled up with laughter.

'Eat my hat!'

* * *

Outside the little farmhouse he stopped the big car. Sue had been running her fingers gently over the walnut dashboard and surreptitiously sniffing the cream leather seats.

'Yes, it really is beautifully made, isn't it?' Edwin's words echoed her immediate thoughts so absolutely that she replied instantly, forgetting her vow to maintain a dignified silence all the way home.

'It certainly is!' she agreed enthusiastically. 'And I can quite see why your uncle chose to keep it as his car. They surely don't make them like this any more.'

'It's probably a good thing they don't; I'd hate to tell you how much petrol she uses, so she's not really a good example in these ecologically conscious days, and her brakes are hardly up to modern standards. One's inclined to forget just how much technology has advanced in modern cars since she was built.'

'Even so, I don't blame you one little bit for keeping her on the road. These seats are the comfiest I've ever sat in!' She knew that the quick way she'd gushed into speech again made it clear that she was trying to keep their conversation on an impersonal level.

Edwin turned to face her, clearly not prepared to follow her lead. 'Are you going to come up to my birthday party on Saturday?'

Caught on the hop, Sue blurted out the truth. 'Do you still want me to?'

'Oh, yes, I want you to, very much...' One of his fingers ran a light outline of her face, and she felt a quiver of tension run through her body with all the force of a forest fire. 'Don't ever be in any doubt of that, my little Victorian miss. I've seen you often enough now to be quite certain...' Very slowly he leant forward until his mouth touched hers, his tongue delicately outlining her lips. As she swayed towards him, he pulled her close, both arms cradling her body to his as he gently forced her lips apart, his tongue beginning to explore the inner heat of her mouth, sending overwhelming waves of sensual pleasure coursing like mad tsunamis through every quivering, receptive nerve of her body. The skilled exploration continued, each delicious plunge bringing intoxicating pleasure in its wake.

She breathed in his subtle perfume, a heady mixture of aftershave mixed with his clean-smelling hair and skin, and her senses began to swim under the rising tide of passion. Never before had she remotely had the sensation of being on the point of losing total control.

It was one of the hardest struggles of her life to fight it, but she knew she had to, she mustn't give in, this was what he wanted, expected...

'Hey...' She dragged her mouth away from his. 'You certainly don't believe in wasting time, do you?' Her voice sounded breathy and small, quite unlike hers normally, as she removed herself as far as possible from his too close proximity. He was dynamite as far as she was concerned! Her whole body felt alive and far too aware of him. Oh, God! How was she to stop him walking all over her if he was able to bring her to her knees by just kissing her?

But maybe he too was having problems controlling his feelings, because he allowed her to turn away from him.

'Well? Will you come to London?' His voice sounded amused and above all certain, as if there could be no doubt.

Sue knew she was caught in a dilemma. Half of her couldn't wait to see him again, but the other half had reservations about just why he wanted to keep in close touch with her. Maybe her blonde looks were an added attraction, but she couldn't forget the light of blazing excitement in his eyes when he'd heard about the picture.

Oh, he was clever! How well he must know that that kiss of his had helped weaken her resolve that it would be safer not to see much of him in the future, in spite of her now strong feelings of delicious danger in his presence.

'That's very kind of you.' She stopped, then came to a lightning decision. 'I accept!' She tried not to hear his relief as he let his breath out in a gentle sigh.

'I'll be in touch about time and place... I wish I could start to work right away on your pictures but I have commitments that I can't get out of, so I'll have to try and arrange another time to come down if you're not prepared to let me take the pictures back to London.'

'You know I won't! We talked about that at dinner.' Sue was quite glad for an excuse to remember just how doubtful she really was about his motives for seeking her out.

'I suppose you're still going to fight about that little picture I bought for you!'

'Look, Edwin, how can I possibly accept that as a present? Why, you're a comparative stranger, and it's nonsense that you owe me anything, you know it is!'

'I don't feel you're a stranger. You're my little goose girl who's grown up...'

Sue was left feeling breathless and even more conscious of danger. She felt as if she was trembling on the edge of a cliff with a drop beneath her of dizzying height. She could let herself fall forward, perhaps to be caught in a pair of strong arms, or she could step back from the brink to safety.

Put like that there really wasn't any choice, was there? Sue took a firm grasp of her bag as her hand fumbled for the door-catch.

'Thank you for a delicious dinner,' she gabbled, intent on getting away as soon as possible, but a lean arm snaked out and a warm hand imprisoned her wrist.

'Don't be frightened! You've no need to run away...' She heard the amusement in his voice and paradoxically that made her angry. She wasn't a child any more, but an experienced woman! She pulled her wrist away from his clasp.

'I know that! What do you think I am? An inexperienced teenager?'

'Not very old.' There was warm amusement in his voice. 'But very beautiful... I shall look forward to seeing you on Saturday and you needn't bring me any present, except your presence!' By this time Sue was standing safely in the tiny front garden of the farmhouse, and she heard him start the big car and drive away into the night.

A weekend in London! Do you know I think I've been rusticating for too long, because I'm really looking forward to it? Sue told herself with a pleased expression as she drove through the suburbs towards Fulham where she was going to stay in a friend's flat.

It had certainly all worked out quite well, she thought as she concentrated on the traffic, Geoffrey and Jane away for the weekend and delighted for her to move in and cat-sit for them.

She rather hoped though that the studio wasn't going to be in the same awful mess it was last time she'd stayed there.

She was going shopping tomorrow morning because she reckoned she deserved something new, and Edwin's party was the perfect excuse to go and buy a wonderful dress. She ignored the prudent inner voice that insisted on warning her there was nothing wrong with her grey silk, telling herself she had had it for ages now and it was time she had something new. She rather thought it should be black and figure-hugging, to set off her blonde looks.

She brought her mind sharply to the present to concentrate more on her driving. She always forgot how much more aggressive people were in London. It didn't do to be too polite at the wheel, and she'd be pleased when she eventually arrived, because she was tired.

Maybe she was tired because she hadn't been sleeping too well since Edwin had left. He'd left her with so many unanswered questions.

First there'd been the blow to hear that he was the expert she'd have to depend on over Gran's pictures. Then, almost more importantly, there was the physical effect he had on her. She might try to expunge those heady moments in his arms but her body wouldn't let her. Even thinking about him was enough to revive memories that the rational half of her definitely thought better hidden if they couldn't be forgotten.

He'd taken away her peace, and that was affecting her ability to work. She found it difficult to concentrate, her mind endlessly slipping away, speculating whether she'd handled things badly by telling him everything.

Perhaps she should have taken more time, letting him see a couple of the pictures, then telling him she had doubts about their authenticity. Unfortunately that wasn't in her nature. She'd never been much good at keeping secrets, disliking the need to keep a guard on her tongue. Not that she'd betray anyone else's, but she just didn't like having them.

Of course she'd studied the pictures herself, but she'd been unable to come to any satisfactory conclusion. Undoubtedly they were painted in the same way that John Tamerton painted, but then, she told herself, of course Augustus would have painted in a similar manner because that was the way he was taught.

It bothered her that for the moment she was unable to decide either way. It seemed that anyone with her job ought to be able to see the fine differences but she was forced to consider the unwelcome fact that she might have been wrong, and that her grandmother might quite simply have kept those pictures because she had liked them the best.

All she could do now was to pray that Edwin would at least consider the possibility seriously, whatever his feelings, because undoubtedly her theory held the best explanation of why her grandmother should have kept them hidden for so long.

So she was in a dreamy frame of mind the following morning when she went shopping. Indeed she allowed the shop assistant to choose a dress for her, and had to admit, once she'd put it on, that it certainly did things for her.

'I knew it was right,' the girl told her, a little smugly, 'when I said black would be wonderful with your hair!' There was a trace of envy behind her words as she looked at Sue's image in the mirror.

'You aren't the first to say that blondes look good in black!' Sue answered. 'I've known that for years, but I have to admit that occasionally I like a change. When I was at college we all went round in black jeans and T-shirts...' She smiled at her memories. Those had been the days! The sort of dress she was wearing now would have been an outrage at most of the parties she'd gone to then. That was when she had first really discovered the heady power of her looks over the opposite sex; fighting off the boys she didn't fancy, and yet, for all her outrageous clothes and behaviour, she'd been remarkably innocent in her fun.

She'd had boyfriends, yes, but none of them had really meant anything to her; that had come later, when she'd first left college. She'd fallen really hard for Justin Poole. In fact you could say that so far he'd been the only serious love of her life. There had been times when she'd wondered if she'd ever again meet anyone she'd fancy half as much. That was why Edwin Ashley had assumed such importance to her so quickly. He had reminded her that she was young, pretty and still alive; reawakened feelings she'd been afraid she'd lost forever when Justin Poole had walked out of her life.

It hadn't mattered that none of her friends had particularly liked him; if anything that had just made the attraction stronger. She'd hoped to marry him, and it had been a shattering blow to discover that her dreams had had no basis in reality.

She'd become so lost in her thoughts that it was quite an effort to come back to the present, and she blinked a little as she heard the girl say, 'I think you could have those straps shortened a bit.' She came to stand behind Sue. 'See what I mean?'

Sue looked critically back at herself in the mirror. The dress, figure-hugging until it flared mid-thigh, the soft chiffon flattering the slightest leg movement, was simple yet sensuous. Yes, she thought, the girl was right; with the straps shortened it would look better. 'It's really "me", isn't it? And I bet it's going to cost a lot more than I can afford!'

'You've got to have it, though, haven't you? I mean if I were you I wouldn't hesitate!' the girl answered eagerly.

Sue remembered that she'd saved herself a thousand pounds by not buying the picture from Edwin, and if she'd been able to afford that then there was really very little reason for not paying out a fraction of that on the dress.

'Well, that's me settled, then!' She smiled back into the salesgirl's eyes. 'OK, I'll take it!'

She walked into the restaurant that Edwin had taken over for the evening confident that she was looking her best. It had been a long time since she'd gone to a party intent on having a good time. Over the years she'd perfected a technique. Arrive late. Stand quite still in the entrance waiting to be noticed, then smile into the eyes of the first man who caught her attention. It had never failed in its impact, and it didn't this evening. Although the room was jam packed with people, the noise level only just bearable, she managed to create a small silence. Enough anyway to guarantee that a great many eyes were avidly studying her as she stood in the doorway, apparently quite oblivious of the attention she was getting.

'So you came after all...' Edwin, looking impossibly handsome in a dinner-jacket, came up to greet her, smiling into her eyes. She raised her brows a little, happy at the unmistakable effect she was having on him.

'Did you doubt I'd turn up?' She smiled back, a cool smile that was full of promise. 'Happy birthday!'

'Yes, I had my doubts. When you want something as much as I did, it's hard to believe one's luck when reality comes to dispel the dreams...' he answered, outrageously, and Sue found it impossible to keep her colour from mounting.

'Dreams are insubstantial things at best, aren't they? At least I've always found them so...'

Edwin gave her an appreciative smile, as if pleased that she was able to keep him at a distance, but he didn't answer directly.

'You look wonderful.' He took her arm and she realised that he intended to keep her at his side as she allowed him to lead her into the thick of the party.

CHAPTER FOUR

EDWIN was so pointed in his attention to her that Sue wasn't sure whether to be flattered or embarrassed. He introduced her to his friends, yet all the time maintaining a distinctly proprietorial manner over her, so that it would have been a brave man who tried to come between them. She was rather forcefully reminded of an old dog her grandmother had owned. He'd displayed very much the same attitude over his bones. One could look and admire, but try to get too close and a fierce growl would remind you who was their owner.

Nor was she made to feel at ease by Georgina Foliot's disapproval. While it was not obviously overt, Sue could feel the other woman's eyes following her every move, and in the manner of such things her own were drawn back for fleeting contact more often than she found comfortable.

Naturally it had to be Georgina who later in the evening appeared at her side with a reminder of her past.

'I didn't realise, Susan, that you were the art student my cousin Justin fell for a couple of years ago...'

This time there was no mistaking the malice in her eyes as Sue turned to look into the blue eyes and handsome face of the one man who'd ever managed to touch her heart.

Just for a moment the past spun back and she was once more under the spell of laughing blue eyes, then the world righted itself. This was the man who despite his professions of love had given her up because his mother hadn't thought her good enough. Those eyes of his were just as blue as she remembered, but this time she was able to stand back, as it were, and look at him as a whole.

'Hello, Susie! You look just as beautiful as I remembered.' The warm, surface charm was there for all to see, but she was pleased that after that first shocked recognition her heart had steadied into its normal rhythm.

'Hello, Justin...' Her glance was cool as she studied the petulant droop to his lips, the slightly receding chin almost with surprise. 'How's your mother?' She hadn't been able to resist that little dig, but was made to regret it as a flush dulled his features.

'My mother died early last year. I thought perhaps you would have seen it in the papers?'

Uncomfortably she shook her head. Why, it seemed as if even from the grave Justin's mother was able to make her feel awkward, to put her in the wrong.

'I don't have time to read those sort of papers,' she answered, wondering if she should make some conventional apologies. As old Lady Poole had been her implacable enemy and been frightfully rude the only time they'd ever met, she thought it would be hypocritical in the extreme to pretend sorrow; anyway, Edwin, who'd been listening silently to this exchange, came to her rescue.

'Poor Justin! What a disappointment it must have been when you didn't get a letter from Sue.'

Sue caught her breath in a little gasp as she took in the thinly veiled sarcasm behind his words.

Justin, obviously put out by Edwin's interjection, ignored it, trying to assert his own claim on her attention.

'I tried to get in touch, Susie, but you'd left the London studio and nobody knew where you'd gone!' he protested. 'In fact one of the chaps was rather rude. He had the cheek to tell me that all your friends knew your address.' It was plain to see that he still felt affronted at being treated like that; also that she was in the wrong for having disappeared so drastically from his life.

'I went back to live with my grandmother,' she answered, her expression still cool and non-committal, but his was full of disbelief.

'You've been living in the country all this time? You told me that it was boring and nothing ever happened there!'

A wry expression twisted her lips. 'Why not? It's where I was brought up after all! And I don't remember saying anything like that; it was you who always said you found it boring! Anyway, what's wrong with living in the country? As I recall you used to spend every weekend there.'

'But you were such a party girl——'

Sue interrupted before he could go any further. 'I still am...' here she smiled at Edwin '...but like most people I've discovered that there are other things that are fun to do as well!' He looked a little disbelieving, so she continued, 'People grow up, you know!'

Georgina now moved in confidently, linking her arm with Edwin's.

'Why don't we leave these two to revive what are obviously happy memories?'

Edwin took one look at Sue's shattered face, and disengaged himself neatly. His eyes danced with amusement as he studied her attempts at concealing her dismay, before returning to smile at Georgina.

'Aren't you a bit out of date, Georgina? Surely you've heard that expression about flogging dead horses? Anyway, one should never look back in life, only forward. I'm right, Sue, aren't I?' Confidently he took hold of her arm in a proprietorial manner again, and Sue, secure with his support, felt able to make polite noises to the pair left behind.

'I'm sorry to hear about your mother; you were very fond of her, I know.' She allowed herself to be swept away by Edwin, just turning to smile over her shoulder and direct her final comment at the two left behind. Justin's face was a picture of stunned disbelief at the way he'd been cut out, while Georgina stood as pale and expressionless as a piece of stone but with a look in her eye that was as merciless as Medusa's of long ago.

Later Georgina came to find her as she was sitting at a table with a couple of other girls. The men had gone off to fetch food from the buffet at one end of the room, and Georgina slid into a vacant seat next to her.

'You shouldn't have allowed Edwin to keep you away from Justin,' she started to say, a false smile just showing up the coldness of her eyes. 'He's never really got over you, you know!'

'No, I don't know,' Sue answered briskly. 'Anyway, if he'd really wanted to get in touch with me again, he'd have done it.'

Georgina shrugged her shoulders. 'Oh, I don't know! Perhaps he had to see you again to realise exactly what he was missing!'

'Ah, but you're forgetting me! As Edwin said, there's no point in looking back through life, and I'd only to see Justin again to wonder what on earth I saw in him. It didn't take long for me to realise that it was only his charm, and because he had a high opinion of himself...' Georgina looked at her intently. 'You're really over him?'

Sue's face lit up with amusement. 'I'm really over him!'

'I hope it isn't a case of out of the frying-pan into the fire?'

Sue stiffened slightly. 'What do you mean?' she hedged.

'Come on, you know perfectly well what I mean! Our host has singled you out for special attention this evening, and I hope you haven't let it go to your head? He's quite a ladies' man, so you're just one in a long line...' She got up with a charming smile as Edwin came back, balancing a couple of plates and two glasses of wine.

'Don't let me drive you away!' he told her, a smile in his eyes.

'I won't!' she smiled back. 'But you needn't worry. I'm being taken care of...'

'Now that I didn't doubt for a minute!' His laughing rejoinder, and the way his eyes appreciated her, made it even clearer to Sue that Georgina's earlier remark about Edwin being a ladies' man could only be based on fact. Not that she was really surprised; anyone who packed such a sexual punch as Edwin Ashley was bound to be experienced with her sex.

All the same, the way he was treating her this evening was heady stuff. She didn't have much difficulty in banishing Georgina and her warnings from her mind as she continued to allow Edwin to monopolise her attention. His eyes were sending her very disturbing messages, and she was receiving those signals loud and clear. Not one of his guests would be left in doubt that he was very interested in her, and they too in turn were intrigued by her.

In spite of herself Sue had been impressed by the people she had met this evening: a large sprinkling of people connected with the art world, from dealers to owners of galleries, some who worked for the two great auction houses, even one or two artists. For the rest there were important clients as well as what she thought of as the more ordinary people like herself who perhaps had been asked because they had been or could be useful to him. She didn't doubt there were genuine friends here as well, but it was also clear that it wasn't a totally private entertainment.

Edwin had explained earlier. 'This is partly business as well as fun, you know. It's a good way of letting different people get to know each other. So often I go to parties where nearly everyone has some connection with just one branch of art. I think it's more fun to mix people with different backgrounds, don't you?'

Sue thought about it for a moment, then said, 'I suppose so. Although I've always found that if a group of people have the same or overlapping interests it tends to make the party go better, but then,' she smiled, 'I've never given a party this big!'

He changed the subject rather abruptly. 'Was Justin Poole a great friend of yours?'

'Yes, he was, but that was all finished some time ago. Looking back on it now I can't imagine why I allowed myself to get fond of him...' she mused, chin in one hand. 'I mean, he's quite good-looking, but he was always a terrible mummy's boy, and I never measured up to what she wanted for her only son!'

He gave her a quick look. 'Did that matter?'

'At the time it hurt, I suppose. I mean, it's not very nice to have to accept that you aren't good enough in someone else's eyes.'

'I've always thought he was a bit of a fool...' Edwin's voice was light, almost casual '...and what you've just told me confirms it.' He slanted her a quick, unreadable look. 'It rather looks as if he's realised that fact and would like to take up where he left off!'

Sue gave him her most bewitching smile. 'He's left it too late. There's never been any point in trying to go back in time; it doesn't work, does it?'

'No, I don't think it does, but then I've never been tempted to try and turn the clock back.' He gave her a slow smile. 'I've always been more interested in trying out new experiences instead of rehashing the past. By the way, I'm hoping to be free for a long weekend at the end of the next week. Is there any chance you could put me up while I look at the pictures?'

'I don't see why not...' She carefully didn't look at him.

'Good. Well, if it's all right I'll be down some time on Friday, probably after lunch.'

'Fine. I'm pleased you're able to come down so quickly.' Once more he looked at her and she was unable to read his expression.

'It's important. Don't forget I've got my retrospective to organise.'

'No, I hadn't forgotten that!' she snapped.

'Now don't get cross! You've been a charming companion all evening so far...'

'Don't push your luck, Edwin! Anyway, I think it's about time you concentrated on some other of your guests, don't you?'

'But suppose I don't want to?' he riposted.

'Then want must be your master!' She stood up gracefully. 'Anyway, you've made enough of an exhibition of me for one evening!'

'You haven't exactly looked as if you've objected!' He too stood up, a lazy smile on his face, so that she was tempted to try and take him down a peg or two!

'I was nicely brought up, haven't you noticed?'

He lounged in front of her, a dangerously sleek male animal at the height of his powers, his hands in his pockets, the white of his dress shirt in contrast to the gleaming dark hair and brows, the warm sherry-brown eyes still sending their disturbing message.

'I think you like to have your own way!'

'Don't you?' She gave him a derisive smile of her own, then walked slowly away, aware that he was watching every step.

Georgina caught up with her in the ladies'. 'I hope this means that you've put Edwin on hold?'

Sue gave her a look of surprise. 'It does, but I still haven't quite worked out what it has to do with you.'

Georgina's pale cheeks flushed with unaccustomed heat. 'I'd have thought you'd have learnt your lesson by now. Haven't you understood that men like Edwin and Justin enjoy having fun with girls like you, but they don't marry them?'

This hit below the belt ensured that she got out of the cloakroom so quickly that she almost knocked another girl flat in the process. She apologised, and tried to control her temper. Well, what a bitch! If she'd stayed near Georgina for one minute longer, she'd have hit her! The cards were down on the table properly now, and as she tried not to brood too seriously on the other woman's words she allowed herself to be monopolised by one of her old art teachers who'd now become surprisingly eminent.

He was telling her about a commission he'd just brought off, and she knew he really just needed a sympathetic ear to tell him how clever he'd been.

'Well done, Jim! I'm so pleased...' Sue turned to give his hand a small squeeze. He looked frightfully pleased with himself as he answered, and she was amused to see that they had attracted Edwin's attention. So, in spite of her warning, he wasn't going to leave her alone after all! After her little session with Georgina she wasn't prepared to make an issue over her bid for freedom any longer. She guessed he was making slow progress towards the two of them, and she was amused to discover that Jim was aware of that fact as well.

'Anyway, if I don't leave you alone, I can see that this just might be the end of my beautiful friendship with Edwin. He's had his eye on us for the last half-hour, and I don't want him putting any ideas into Mary's head!'

Sue smiled. 'Do you think so?'

'As if you didn't know, you beguiling little witch! I'm on my way...' He picked up one of her hands and placed a kiss on it, before melting away into another group of people near by.

'Don't tell me he's another old acquaintance?' Edwin demanded.

'He was one of my art teachers at college,' she answered demurely.

'Do you have any other acquaintances here?' he queried with one of his lazy smiles. She debated whether to tell him the truth or not, her head a little on one side as she looked at him.

'Why the inquisition, Edwin? Just because I've turned up as your guest tonight doesn't give you any rights over me!' This provocative little speech didn't have quite the effect she intended.

'Don't try to deny it, Sue. You're as keen to get to know me better as I am you!'

Now this was plain speaking with a vengeance. Also he was going too fast for her. Sue raised her eyebrows slightly. 'You're taking an awful lot for granted, aren't you? So OK, this is your birthday, but don't run away with the idea that I'm one of your presents, because I'm not!'

'So fierce a denial!' His voice had dropped to a silky purr. 'Suppose I decided to put that to the test?'

She backed away, alarmed. 'You wouldn't! Not here, not in front of everyone!'

'Don't be too sure! You're the image of your Victorian grandmother. Don't you know that it has become an overwhelming obsession of mine to test out all those erotic possibilities that are so explicit in that last, great picture of her?' The brooding sensuality of his expression, the slightly flaring nostrils, the full lower lip as he allowed his eyes to strip her, was one of the most exciting yet somehow frightening experiences of her life. Here they both were, in a room full of people, yet they might have been alone. She was enclosed with him in the web of sexual tension that he had woven so expertly and so easily around her.

As her feelings of panic, half delightful, half shameful, threatened to engulf her, she made a last, desperate attempt to escape. She turned rather blindly away from him to find salvation in one of that evening's acquaintances. Luckily oblivious to the vibrations that seemed to spark off each of them, she was offered a chance to run away.

'Sue! There's talk about going on to Tramp to dance. Are you on?' One of her companions on the table where she'd sat for dinner was at her side.

'Why not?' Sue grasped at this offer as if she were in danger of drowning. Edwin had already singled her out for special attention in front of his friends. The thought that he might be tempted to make his pursuit even more obvious filled her with an uncomfortable mix of feelings of which the topmost was her conviction that here was neither the time nor the place.

No doubt if she kept away from Edwin Georgina would be happy, and, while Georgina's happiness wasn't of paramount importance, trying to keep herself prepared to repel the next attack from her was becoming a bit of a bore, because Sue could feel that basilisk stare of hers beginning to bore holes in her back. It would be better to get out and get away, somewhere, anywhere, where she could sort out her jumble of feelings and emotions.

Inevitably Justin again attached himself to her, and Sue found that she was far too interested in her own problems to take him seriously; anyway, she didn't really have the heart to repulse him too severely. He'd hurt her so much in the past that she'd once thought she'd never be able to forgive him, but now she just found him rather pathetic in his attempts to ingratiate himself with her. If her eyes did rather too often check the rooms for Edwin's presence, at least her goodwill made her accept Justin's presence with a fairly good grace. He was her saviour from a situation she'd found she couldn't control, and as long as Georgina left them alone then she wasn't going to complain. He didn't seem even to know that he had only half her attention, but she found it possible to listen to him with only half an ear.

Her wary eyes were continuously checking that Edwin kept his distance. He'd let her go so easily that she wondered if he too had decided that discretion should be their master. She'd had the impression that he'd been dangerously near to losing control in those final few minutes before they'd been interrupted.

Just before the group of them left to go on to the nightclub, Edwin came to find her again. 'I see you've decided to let bygones by bygones.' He nodded in Justin's direction, not looking best pleased. Sue decided that at all costs the mood must be kept light between them.

'More likely it's your delicious champagne!' she answered lightly. 'I just don't feel like having a fight tonight. Anyway,' she shrugged, 'as long as he doesn't bug me too much, who cares?'

'Well, if you don't, who indeed?' he agreed smoothly. 'But I shouldn't encourage him too much. He's the type that if you give him an inch he takes——'

But she interrupted crossly, 'You don't need to warn me what he's like! I went out with him for nearly two years.'

'What a waste. I should have thought you could have done much better for yourself than that!'

Her eyes glinted up at him under their curved lids. 'Aren't you forgetting something?' Her voice was deceptively mild. 'They say love is blind!' She turned to leave, but his arm snaked out and caught her by the wrist. He pulled her back, so that her body was pressed close to his, and, ignoring everyone around them, his head came lower so that she could feel his breath on her neck.

'Let me go, Edwin!' Her cheeks had become flushed under the curious and amused glances that danced fleetingly over them before good manners ensured that they moved on to other objects of interest or amusement.

'Not till I've said all I want!' His voice had become dangerously low. 'Don't get mixed up again with Justin Poole just because you've got too kind a heart to give him the push. He's not the sort of man who could ever make you happy...'

She spun round in his loosened grip. 'What right do you think you have to tell me what I can and can't do?'

'I don't think you're ready to hear just yet!' His whole expression was now full of laughter, as if he realised he might have put his foot in his mouth, but didn't particularly care one way or the other.

She gave him a brooding, rather considering look. 'I don't like being told what to do by a comparative stranger.'

'Ouch!' he winced, with pretended pain. 'Don't forget it's still my birthday.' Lilting amusement in his face had her accepting that he'd recovered more easily than she had from the strong emotions of their last encounter.

'Only just, Edwin. Another couple of minutes and it'll all be over!' She bit her lip before giving him a social smile. 'It's been a fantastic party. Thanks for asking me...' She held out her hand. 'I'll look forward to seeing you next Friday.' And that was a lie if ever there was one! Out of all the mixture of emotions and feelings that seethed beneath her deceptively calm exterior, their next meeting lay like a lowering thundercloud over everything. If she allowed that meeting to go forward unchaperoned, she knew it would be her personal doomsday. He would devour her, body and soul, like some hungry lion, and she would be incapable of stopping him from taking everything he wanted unless she could find some hidden source of strength in the coming week.

'But not as much as I'll be looking forward to seeing you again...' His eyes were promising her—well, she didn't want to admit to herself that she found his message intolerably exciting, so she kept her distance, just faintly lifting her brows as if to show him that she doubted his sincerity.

She was sleepy and disinclined to think too carefully about Edwin's behaviour towards her at his birthday party as she drove back to Devon the next day. She tried successfully to concentrate on her driving and not to allow Edwin to monopolise her thoughts.

Sheer perversity had ensured that she'd allowed Justin to dance with her, as he'd made sure he was included in the party that went on to the nightclub. Although she'd tried to make it clear to him that there was no chance of his picking up where he'd left off, so to speak, he'd appeared to ignore her warnings. She wasn't totally convinced that she'd succeeded, particularly as she came to realise that he had indeed a very high opinion of himself and his ability to attract women. When he'd asked for her address, she'd refused to give it to him, telling him, 'There's no point, Justin. I'm not interested in seeing you again!'

The blue eyes looked deeply into her own. 'I see you're still angry with me. Why don't you let me take you out to dinner and explain what happened?'

'No, Justin! Anyway, you've no need to make any explanations. Your mother did it for you!'

For a moment he looked as if he couldn't believe his ears. 'Mother?' he repeated.

'Yes. She told me I wasn't good enough for your family.' He looked so disconcerted, and so angry, that she couldn't help laughing at him. 'Cheer up, Justin! It didn't matter, because I agree with her.'

'She'd no right to interfere!' he spluttered, then appeared to pull himself together. 'I'm sorry, baby! She got a bit difficult in her old age, and found it hard to accept that times had changed. I know that if she'd had the chance to get to know you she'd have changed her mind!'

'I doubt it!' Sue once more in her mind's eye saw the martial and imposing Lady Poole. 'Anyway, it doesn't matter because she was right after all. You and I were not suited, and that's all there is to it. I'm not interested any more, Justin...'

He gave her a darkling look. 'I suppose it's Edwin Ashley you've got your eye on. Well, let me tell you——'

'Justin! I won't let you tell me anything. Please get it into your thick head that I'm not interested in you, and I'm definitely not interested in raking over the ashes to see if a small flame is still there.'

He gave her a brooding, sulky glare. 'Georgina looks on Edwin Ashley as her property. I should watch out if I were you; she doesn't like losing out, she never did, even as a child!' he told her nastily.

'So? I can't see that your cousin, or her boss, is any concern of mine!' Sue treated him to a look of disdain. 'Why don't you get on with your own little life and stop jumping to conclusions about mine?'

'Does that mean you're not interested in Edwin?' he began eagerly.

'It means mind your own business!' she finally snapped, and purposefully ignored him for the rest of the night.

All the same the news about Georgina and Edwin had made her heart sink lower and lower as she tried to make sense of Edwin's singling her out. They always said that actions were supposed to speak louder than words, didn't they? And Edwin's actions had been—well, she'd have to be an idiot not to realise that he was interested in her. No wonder Georgina had been so angry. It couldn't have been much fun for her to have to stand back and watch him hanging around her for most of the evening.

Nearly home! she told herself with relief as she swung her small car into the narrow track that led round to the back of the farmhouse. It took her some time to realise that something was out of place as she got out of the car, her face puzzled.

The studio door was open. She knew she'd locked it before leaving, but maybe Bridget had come back. Of course, that had to be the explanation!

'Bridget? Where are you? I'm home...' But there was no answer. She slowly walked over to the studio.

'I don't believe it!' Every painting that had been stacked around the walls looked as if it had been checked then discarded into untidy heaps, and there was a gap on the wall. It didn't take her long to find out what she already half expected. The unsigned Tamertons and her copy of her grandmother with the goats had disappeared.

Hardly waiting a second, she spun on her heel and ran towards the house. The back door had been lifted off its hinges and was propped uselessly against the wall. Holding back her sobs of outrage, she ran quickly through the house and up to her bedroom, which was dominated by a large and old-fashioned wooden bed. Quickly she leant down before finally getting on her knees, lifting up the heavy linen valance to look underneath, then breathed a sigh of relief. They hadn't found it!

The hiding place that her grandmother had kept the painting in, the wooden drawer that ran the length of the bed quite separate from the bed base, hadn't been touched. She bent her head on to the mattress, offering a silent prayer of thanks before getting to her feet to run downstairs.

Her anxious eyes looked around her home, checked each room, but nothing else appeared to have been taken, not even her Tamerton watercolours. Sue sat down on the bottom step of the stairs, and rested her hands in her chin.

Funny thieves, she told herself. They take my pictures but leave behind the TV and the video, let alone the bits of Gran's silver... And wasn't it all a bit too much of a coincidence? This was the first time for months that she'd left the house empty. Edwin Ashley's birthday invitation had come a mite too pat in view of what had happened, hadn't it?

She jumped up, ready to call the police. She had strong doubts that they'd be able to do anything, but she had to try. First of all, though, she'd have to call Bridget. Maybe she knew something about this puzzle.

'My dear!' Bridget had sunk down into a chair, her brows drawn together in a worried frown. It hadn't taken her long to come over to the house. 'You can't think that Edwin Ashley had anything to do with this!' Her hand gestured. 'At least promise me you'll not mention his name to the police?'

Sue gave her an impatient look. 'Of course I won't! They'd never be able to find any proof that he was behind it, but think, Bridget! Who else had the slightest motive, or knowledge? If only I hadn't mentioned my ideas about Augustus Frome to him, but I did! He was the one who told me that I could damage John Tamerton's reputation by even thinking of questioning his work!'

'What about your cousins? You told me they were pretty upset at being left out of your grandmother's will.'

She dismissed them with a casual wave of her hand. 'Why should they ever have heard of Augustus Frome? Anyway, it's too pat, Bridget! OK, I might have been suspicious if it had happened earlier, but just now! Somebody had to know I would be away.' Bridget was left silent as Sue busied herself ringing up their local police station.

Later, much later, when the local CID and Bridget had gone, Sue was left to mull over her own thoughts. A local carpenter had come in and mended the doors, which Sue had thought was pretty good going on a Sunday until she got the bill. The police had calmed her down, telling her her insurance company would pay, while Bridget had laughed at her indignation.

'What did you expect? The poor chap probably had to give up his session in the pub, as well as leave his family for Sunday lunch. Of course he wants to be paid double time! Anyway, would you want to have been left with the doors unmended until tomorrow?'

That had made Sue shiver; indeed once she started she found she couldn't stop, one of the detectives warning her that she was in shock.

She had gone to sit in the kitchen with Bridget, who had made her some tea, which the detective had recommended. Neither of them knew any other cure for shock. 'I can't believe——' Bridget had spoken in a low voice '—that Edwin Ashley would have anything to do with this!'

Sue had shut her eyes in anguish.

'You don't know how much money he may have tied up in Tamertons. If their value fell he could lose a fortune!'

'Even so, from what you've told me he doesn't strike me as someone prepared to behave like this. I think of him—I can't help it, dear!—I think of him as an honourable man.'

'You don't even know him!' Sue had protested. 'Anyway, you try to give me another reason, then,' she'd answered, her voice tired and dispirited.

'I think it has to be a coincidence, and that your nasty cousins have somehow set it up. Hey!' She had sat up a little straighter. 'Do you think the burglar would have come in even if you'd been here?'

Sue had shaken her head. 'No, of course I don't! No one would be so stupid. No, this has to have something to do with Edwin, I just know it has!' she'd finished in a fierce whisper. Bridget had just sat and looked miserable.

It had been a tiring day in more ways than one, and Sue longed for oblivion to block out her too active thoughts as she lay in her bed. She tossed and turned, but sleep stubbornly refused to come. It seemed unkind of fate to have pushed Justin back into her life and at the same time to have given her more pain than she would have believed possible from finding that his possible replacement in her heart had feet of clay.

Half of her had always had reservations, not quite trusting herself to believe that this stranger could be so important to her on such short acquaintance, but he was, and the pain of finding out that he was not to be trusted had been surprisingly sharp. If only. Two of the saddest words in the English language, because he would have been so perfect for her. They shared a love and knowledge of Victorian art, and he was one of the most physically attractive men she'd ever met.

She lay back in her grandmother's bed and looked up at the dark ceiling. 'Maybe,' she told herself aloud, 'I've been lucky. Suppose we'd really had a chance of getting close to each other?' She gave a great sigh, and tears rolled down her face. She'd been fighting him ever since they first met. Fighting him because she was terrified of the power she knew he had over her. There had only been kisses to regret, but it had been enough to show her her heart.

'Why?' she asked herself savagely. 'Am I fated to fall for the wrong man?' But even that question didn't help, when the other half of her was still protesting loudly that he was the right man. She tried to concentrate on Georgina's warning of last night: that he was a womaniser, that she was just one girl in a long line. Then there was Justin, telling her that Georgina had set her heart on him. At the end of the party last night she had been rather looking forward to giving Georgina a run for her money...

It was no good; she sat up and turned on the bedside light. Sleep was impossible, and she had a letter to write. She got out of bed to collect her Victorian writing slope, then returned with it, pulling the duvet up high to stop herself feeling chilled.

Dear Edwin,

Your party last night was the greatest and I really enjoyed myself. It was very kind of you to have asked me, particularly as I am such a new acquaintance...

That sounded ridiculously pompous, but did she really care? Once more she picked up her pen.

Sadly on returning home I had a shock. I found I had been burgled. The thief took the four unsigned pictures of my grandmother's, also my copy of the goat girl. Therefore there is now little point in your coming down here next weekend.

Once again, thank you for a wonderful party.

She bit the top of her pen as she tried to think of how to end it, then just wrote her name. 'Sue'.

She took out an envelope, folded the letter and put it in and sealed it. She gave an enormous yawn as she got out of bed again to put her wooden writing slope away, then turned out the light and tried once more to sleep.

His image swam in front of her closed eyes, his dinner-jacket and dress shirt setting off his dark good looks. Oh, that lazy smile as he looked down at her, what warmth in those sherry-brown eyes! How could he have betrayed her? She wished she were an animal so that she could have bayed her misery to the world. Instead she buried her face in her pillow, trying to shut out his image.

She forced herself to think about her lost pictures. They were insured, yes, but she didn't think she'd get the market value for them as Tamertons, and that was her fault. She'd been advised, after her grandmother's death, to take out special insurance to cover them, but the price quoted had been so prohibitive that she'd felt it was an expense she couldn't really afford, so they'd been left covered only under the general contents of the house.

She began to get angry all over again. It was such a clever pre-emptive strike Edwin had made, and so ingenious of him to have cut the ground from under her feet like that. He must have been afraid that she was right after all with her story about Augustus Frome. Somehow she must get her own back. He mustn't be allowed to get away with it. It was bad enough that she couldn't accuse him point-blank, that she had to pay lip-service to convention and the law. She lay back on the pillows and began to weave plans as she allowed her thirst for revenge to consume her.

CHAPTER FIVE

SUE posted her letter the next morning, but although she waited, strung almost unbearably tight by tension, she heard nothing over the next few days. From having been full of a sort of furious anticipation, her last hope of his innocence vanished with his surprising silence.

Where was he? He must have had her letter by now, so why hadn't he rung her? She found it impossible to accept that he didn't know about her burglary. Her emotions were on a see-saw of anger and hurt mixed up with bewildered humiliation at what she saw as his betrayal of her and her interests.

She threw herself into her work with single-minded concentration, as if by doing so she could escape from her problems. She refused to allow herself to think about anything that wasn't of immediate importance, and in consequence managed to finish another of her copies a whole week earlier than planned. That left her by late Friday morning with nothing to do.

In desperation she weeded and tidied the tiny piece of garden in front of the farmhouse. She was on her knees, trying to pull up a particularly resistant clump of weeds right at the back of one of the narrow borders when she heard a car pull up and stop outside in the lane. She tried to stand up in a hurry, and got caught up in a tangle of rambling rose which instead of busily climbing the house had now somehow got

PLAY THE
LUCKY CARNIVAL WHEEL
and get as many as
SIX FREE GIFTS..

HOW TO PLAY:

1. With a coin, carefully scratch away the silver panel opposite. Then check your number against the numbers opposite to find out how many gifts you're eligible to receive.

2. You'll receive brand-new Mills & Boon Romances and possibly other gifts - ABSOLUTELY FREE! Return this card today and we'll promptly send you the free books and the gifts you've qualified for!

3. We're sure that, after your specially selected free books. you'll want more of these heartwarming Romances. So unless we hear otherwise, every month we will send you our 6 latest Romances for just £1.90 each * - the same price in the shops. Postage and Packing are free - we pay all the extras!
* Please note prices may be subject to VAT.

4. Your satisfaction is guaranteed! You may cancel or suspend your subscription at any time, simply by writing to us. The free books and gifts remain yours to keep.

NO COST! NO RISKS!
NO OBLIGATION TO BU

caught in her jersey and was disintegrating into a messy and painful tangle around her.

'Stand still!' Sue stopped swearing, her whole body suddenly unnaturally immobile as she recognised that deep, amused voice. 'Damn! I hope you're going to offer me danger money, Sleeping Beauty, this thing's vicious!'

Now that was something he didn't need to tell her! Did he really think she'd stay crouched in this deeply unnatural position unless she had to? 'Edwin?'

He heard the uncertainty in her voice. 'Who else were you expecting?' There was a tiny silence, leaving her without anything to say. He couldn't still be expecting to stay down here with her for the weekend, could he? 'Nearly there! Of course it would be quicker if I could cut the whole thing away...'

'Don't do that!' Her voice sounded a little strangled.

'OK...' His voice sounded full of amusement again as he continued, 'I suppose you'll be wanting it attached back to the wall once you're free?'

'Well, I certainly can't leave it in a mess, can I?' she answered, her voice tart as she realised how ridiculous she must look. 'But don't worry, I'll get old Bill to come and do it. He knows I'm hopeless up a ladder...' She managed, under instructions, to wriggle free, absurdly conscious of her old torn jeans, and her filthy hands, while he looked as immaculate as if he'd just changed into his clothes.

Edwin pulled her to her feet, his hands taking determined hold of hers, despite her attempts to keep her distance. His eyes laughed down at her as he took in the tangled hair, the scratches, the liberal amount of earth that clung to her. 'I would never have guessed that you were such a child of nature!' he teased. 'But I hope you're pleased to see me?' There was a demanding arrogance in his voice that reminded her of his behaviour at his party, almost as if he'd somehow laid claim to her, that she now belonged to him, but the laugh left his face quickly as he took in her shattered expression.

She swallowed. 'Didn't you get my letter?'

'Letter? No, I haven't seen any letters; I've been up North working out what pictures may have to be sold from an estate that's going to be liable for death duties. I left home on the Sunday after the party.' He frowned down at her. 'What's wrong, Sue?'

She pulled away from him, bending over to collect her gardening equipment, which she piled into the trug she had been using for her weeding.

'Then you won't know... Edwin, there's little point in your remaining here.' Her grey eyes now looked calmly into his puzzled brown ones. 'When I got back here last Sunday I discovered there'd been a break-in. The four oils I showed you the other day, plus my copy of the girl with the goats, have been stolen...'

Now she could have sworn that was genuine puzzlement on his face, as well as anger, but that couldn't be right, could it? She felt a wave of rage sweep through her at his disingenuousness, then bit her lip in a frantic effort of control. She mustn't lose her temper with him.

'You've had the police?' Even his voice sounded shocked, and once more she couldn't help genuinely doubting that he could know until common sense returned.

He had to be behind it, she reiterated savagely but silently to herself. Then, 'Oh, yes, but they don't hold out much hope, you see, because they took so little, not bothering with Gran's silver or the TV and video; they think they were professionals. You know, the ones that steal to order...'

'But who could know about those pictures?' he burst out.

'Exactly!' There was a good deal of meaning in her voice, but heroically she kept her expression non-committal. In the rather fraught silence that followed she braced herself for further ordeals. 'You'd better bring the car around the back. Shall I make you some tea? I'm about to have some myself.'

'Thanks...' He looked thoughtful but also slightly wary, as if he was aware he was walking on thin ice. Once round the corner of the house, Sue leant against the solid stone and shut her eyes. Please, God, don't let me lose my temper! she pleaded silently, knowing that Edwin's presence here was provoking emotions that surged inside her rather like the molten magma of a volcano just before it exploded. Heavy, yet fiery, she could feel them heaving inside her as she strove to control her burning sense of injustice.

Later, as they sat opposite each other at the kitchen table, she could feel him studying her, as if trying to work out what she was thinking.

'You appear to be taking this very calmly. I take it you were properly insured?'

Sue shook her head. 'No, I'm afraid not. I was advised to, after my grandmother's death, but I thought the premiums too heavy so decided to leave it as it always had been.'

'But good God! Those paintings of yours might have fetched anything between twelve and fifteen thousand pounds on the open market!'

She gave him a straight look. 'You think so? I rather doubt it myself because they aren't signed, and they will have no provenance. Anyway, as I've told you, I'm not completely sure they are Tamertons...' There! Why not take the bull by the horns? If he'd arranged to have them taken because of her belief they were painted by Augustus Frome, then she'd show him! She'd already decided on her plan of revenge, and hoped he'd feel guilty enough to go along with it. Well, actually she didn't have much doubt that he would because the bait she proposed to offer would be too much for him to refuse.

'I admit I only saw them quickly, but I have a trained eye. Whoever painted those pictures was no amateur, and I don't think the prospective purchasers would have much difficulty in having them accredited to Tamerton because the subjects are so typical of his work!'

She looked up at him quickly. 'Do you think they'll be sold?'

'I should say undoubtedly, but not in this country — that would be too dangerous.'

'Oh!' She dropped her eyes again.

'Who knew you were going to be away in London?' His voice sounded light, but there was a glimmer of shrewd understanding in his eyes. She shrugged her shoulders lightly.

'No one really, apart from you, that is! Oh, and also the couple who lent me their studio for the weekend...'

'How very awkward for us all!' His voice still sounded light but now there was definite comprehension in his face. 'I suppose, as far as you are concerned, I'm under suspicion?'

This time Sue kept her eyes firmly glued to a knot in the old wooden table, and moved her shoulders in an almost infinitesimal shrug. 'The police asked me the same question...' She left her sentence open.

'And did you oblige with my name?' he queried smoothly.

'No, of course I didn't!' She looked up then and met his eyes.

'I wonder why not?' he mused, but the underlying sarcasm got to her.

'Because I didn't want a writ for libel slapped on me! Even if...' She stopped for a moment, desperate to find the right words, then started again. 'What the police referred to as the "prime instigator" probably had nothing to do with the actual theft. They told me there are so many rackets going on in the art world that it was most unlikely, in the circumstances, that I'd ever see my pictures again; that they'd probably been "stolen to order" or something like that.' She gave a sigh. 'Oh, well, I suppose I've got to be grateful for small mercies. They didn't find the original painting of Gran with the goats, even if they thought they had!'

He leant back in his chair, with what she thought was relief. 'Now that would be difficult to sell!'

Once more Sue kept her eyes on the scrubbed wooden top of the table. 'At least it's brought one thing home to me. I realise now that I can't keep it hidden here any longer; it's too dangerous!' She looked up to meet his ironical gaze. 'I wonder if you'd consider keeping it for me? You could use it in your retrospective, couldn't you? Always supposing you could find room for it.' She had the satisfaction of seeing that he was utterly flabbergasted by her suggestion, indeed could hardly believe his ears.

She sat back in her chair watching him with a faint smile on her face. 'Well? Do you think it's a good idea? If not then I'll have to make other arrangements...'

Just for moment his eyes blazed with such a light that she could hardly bear to look at him. He leaned forward as if to take her hand, hesitated a moment, then withdrew it, saying, 'Thank you!' There was such heartfelt sincerity behind the words that poor Sue's heart leapt a little in her chest with anguish. Thanks to her he thought his retrospective was going to be one of the key events of the year, and so it was, but not quite in the way he thought!

'I suppose you'd like to see it?' She knew her voice sounded a little dead and lacking in enthusiasm but how was she supposed to help it when she hurt so inside? He was looking at her curiously, as if trying to work out her thoughts.

'You know I would! But I have to confess that I'm also intrigued to know just how your grandmother managed to hide it so successfully all these years, because it is quite a large painting, isn't it?'

'Yes, it is large; nearly six feet long by three feet in width.'

He gave a low whistle. 'And did your burglars come into the house? As I recall all the other paintings were kept out in the studio, weren't they?'

'Yes, they did, and yes... They weren't framed, you see; I don't think they ever had been.'

'And they took nothing from the house at all?' His voice was still curious.

'Absolutely nothing, that's what's so extraordinary. They didn't take my watercolours or anything, just those four pictures and my copy.'

'If I remember correctly you told me you hadn't discussed your—er—opinion that Frome was responsible for them with anyone else?'

'Only Bridget, my grandmother's old housekeeper, and she'd never have mentioned it to anyone else, I'm sure!' she finished rather belligerently, she had to admit.

'So as far as you knew, only you, your housekeeper Bridget and myself knew about them, is that right?' Her clear grey eyes couldn't hide their faintly accusing light as she faced him, aware that he was watching her with a slight frown. 'So why are you trusting me with the most important picture of them all?' He slipped that question in so neatly that if she hadn't been prepared for it maybe she would have betrayed herself, but her grey eyes looked limpid and clear as she met his questioning gaze.

'Several reasons!' She rested her chin on her hand, but her eyes still held his. 'First, you're the expert on John Tamerton's work, so I know you'll take great care of it. Also, I shall want you to look at it and see if you think that more than one hand painted it. I've been studying it all week and I shall be interested to hear your conclusions and to see if they coincide with my own. And thirdly, well, why not? You seemed to be really intrigued by it...'

'Is that all?'

Now why should he look faintly disappointed? She let her surprise show. 'Isn't it enough?'

He shrugged a little, then smiled at her. 'I'm sorry, I don't mean to sound ungracious; it's just that I'm surprised, you see.'

She gave him a quick smile, then stood up. 'If you want to satisfy your curiosity, then follow me.' She took him into her bedroom, aware that he was looking around curiously, almost as if he was looking for clues to her character by her surroundings, then she chided herself for being unduly fanciful. As she leant by the bed, lifting the valance to show the narrow cavity beneath the springs of the base, he came and knelt with her.

'How ingenious!' he laughed in a low voice. 'Now who would have expected that?'

'Yes, it was a clever idea, wasn't it? I don't know whether she thought of it herself, or bought the bed with that secret drawer in place.' Edwin, obviously containing his excitement with difficulty, looked at the wood carefully.

'I think she would have had this made specially. Look, the wood is different for a start...' He ran his hands gently along the front of it, before slowly opening the long, narrow drawer. He drew in his breath sharply as the picture was slowly revealed in the afternoon light. Sue helped him pull it free, then he stood it up, balanced it against a chest of drawers, and walked back to admire it.

Sue, inured to the picture's charm by familiarity, watched his face instead, knowing that his whole being was concentrated so fiercely on what he was looking at that she was, for the moment, safe.

He was dressed casually in narrow jeans, black leather riding boots and a loose blue linen shirt with patch pockets. A multicoloured striped wool gabardine jacket finished off the whole trendy outfit and he looked absolutely stunning. In fact nothing could have been in greater contrast to her own definitely shabby clothes, but then she hadn't been expecting him, had she? If she'd known he was going to show up, then she'd have made sure she wasn't dressed like... Hey, wait a minute! She succeeded in reining in her unruly thoughts. What did it matter what she looked like? The man lounging so carelessly next to her in her bedroom had his mind on other and greater things. Now he'd succeeded in getting his own way as far as Gran's picture was concerned she had a feeling that she'd soon lose her importance to him. She was brought smartly back to attention when he turned to speak to her.

'It's even better than I hoped it would be! I think this has to be his masterpiece. What do you think?' His whole face was alive under his passionate interest, and she found herself wondering what it would be like to have that interest focused entirely on oneself. Once more she had to collect her thoughts.

'What? Oh, yes... It's a wonderful picture.'

'You know, you really are remarkably like your grandmother. If I didn't know it wasn't possible, I'd say this could be a portrait of you when you were younger...'

Sue looked at it, frowning a little.

'I don't think we were really all that alike, you know...'

He smiled at her. 'You could only have known her when she was a comparatively old lady. I think if you'd met her when she was young you might have had a shock!'

'Actually I'm supposed to look like my mother!' She was beginning to get a bit uptight at this obsession of his.

'Really? Don't you know?' His eyes were already back studying the picture.

'No, I don't! She left my father when I was three years old, so I've got no memory of her at all.'

'How sad...' He flicked her a quick glance. 'At least you were lucky enough to have your grandmother take care of you. I imagine that must have been better for you than a stepmother or a series of nannies?'

'You seem to have quite a fixation about my grandmother,' Sue commented, feeling a little as if she was poking a wasp's nest with a stick.

'Of course!' He slanted a smile at her. 'Didn't I tell you that my picture of her with the geese is my favourite?'

'Yes, but why is it your favourite?' she persisted.

'Because I thought she was the most enchanting little girl I'd ever seen!' was the prompt response. 'And you yourself, with this——' he gestured with a hand towards the picture '—just confirms my belief that she continued to grow up to be as beautiful as all that early promise implied!'

Sue was left without a word to say and increased colour in her cheeks. Her blood seemed to be flowing through her veins at a greater speed than normal, making her feel a little light-headed at his words. So, she was the living embodiment of a small girl who'd caught his fancy, was she? Well, he'd soon find out she was no prim Victorian miss ready to swoon at his feet! Oh, no! She was going to avenge the theft of her pictures.

'Shall we bring it down to the studio? I think if you're going to look at it properly you're going to need the light, aren't you?'

'Mmm...' He stood silent, as if he could hardly bear to tear his eyes away from it.

'Edwin!' She crossed her arms, impatience written large on her face. She wanted him out of her bedroom. It was bad enough her subconscious tormenting her with his image, let alone her conscious mind having something so readily available to draw on.

'OK! No! I'll take it...' Acutely aware of his possessive instincts as far as the picture was concerned, she stood back to let him pass, trying to keep her resentment in check. It wasn't good for any girl's ego to be compared to somebody on canvas and found wanting. If he found Gran so fascinating as a child then he ought, if he was to be believed about her likeness to her, to be feeling something rather special about her. It was a shame that her reality wasn't going to live up to his dreams, but it definitely helped her to get her emotions under a tighter control. If he'd really fancied her, just her, then he wouldn't be quite so obsessed with the picture, would he? That unanswerable piece of logic helped her to get her feelings about him into perspective again.

All the same she was disconcerted to discover that he certainly intended to spend the weekend with her. She left him alone to gloat in the studio, unable to bear to watch him any longer, but it wasn't long before he followed her back into the house.

'Which is my room?' he asked. 'I thought I'd take my bag up now if you don't mind. There are a couple of things I need for looking at the canvas more closely...' He gave her a radiant smile.

'But... I mean, now the other pictures aren't here. I didn't think you'd be coming this weekend!' she finished in a burst of candour. The change in his expression was almost ludicrous.

'You want me to go away, to leave?'

'Well...' She gestured rather hopelessly with one hand. 'I mean, I'm here alone...'

'But I thought you trusted me!' he protested.

'No! Well, yes, of course I do, as far as the picture is concerned...'

'But you don't trust me as a man, is that right?' He looked dangerously compelling as he leant against the door, just his eyes watching every expression that chased over her face. She swung away from him.

'I don't know you well enough... Anyway, your behaviour at your party...' She felt him walk over, to stand close to her, and her heart began to accelerate uncomfortably.

'But you didn't show much signs of minding, did you?' His voice was low, seductive, soft, and she couldn't stop a quiver running through her whole body. She stiffened, suddenly rigid, as his hand gently swept across the exposed nape of her neck, then she felt his lips burn against her skin. She closed her eyes, desperately praying for strength to resist this practised approach, as he laughed deep in his throat and pulled her round to face him.

'You're so beautiful, my lovely... Don't you know that ever since I've met you you've tormented my dreams?' She could smell the strong male scent of him, and it weakened her senses. His hands gently moulded her face, and she could feel his soft breath on her cheeks.

'I knew, the first moment I laid eyes on you, that you were mine,' he breathed. 'So much the embodiment of a dream that I couldn't believe my luck! Then I found out who you were, and of course that made the whole thing even more of a fantasy, a dream come true! How many men can truly say they've met the girl of their dreams? A warm living being, with lips that beg to be kissed...' His mouth gently, fleetingly found hers. 'With hair as gold as a harvest moon...' She felt his hands, light as butterflies, stroke the contours of her head, then his fingers run through the thick, silky fineness that tumbled so becomingly around her face.

'A body...' his hands moved lower, to slip under her old jersey, then cupped her breasts, his thumbs gently rubbing their hardened nipples '... more exciting than any I dreamed of...' She could feel the heat of him slowly inflaming her senses; she was drowning; if he kissed her she would be lost. She found she was chanting silently to herself. Please, please, please... But she no longer even knew what she was begging for. All her senses were totally concentrated on herself and her surprise at what effect this stranger's gentlest touch could have on her. There was no fear, no holding back, just a sense of absolute rightness that she should be responding so uncharacteristically to his sensuous stroking movements.

But that elusive, magical enchantment was broken before she was bound forever to him by the sensuous silkiness of giving and receiving love. Broken by a mundane, prosaic noise. There were no triumphant trumpets to sound her chastity, just the front doorbell, reinforced by heavy thuds from the knocker.

They broke apart, both looking equally bewildered at their return to the ordinary, everyday world. Guilt at her shameless behaviour had Sue recovering the quickest. Full of self-loathing for what she had so nearly allowed to happen, she half ran towards the front door, impatient to let in her saviour.

'Constable Gibbons, Miss Rivers...' The tall and lanky shape of their local policeman filled the narrow old doorway. Sue gave him a shaky smile, then stood aside to let him come in. He undid his helmet, and holding it under his arm followed her back towards the sitting-room.

'I'm sorry to disturb you——' he started to say, but Sue interrupted him.

'No! You weren't disturbing anything,' she gabbled a little too quickly, and blushed as she saw his surprise. 'Do sit down. Can I get you anything? Tea or coffee?'

'You're very kind, miss, but I'm due back for my tea after this visit, so I'll wait if you don't mind.'

'No, of course...' She heard the door open behind her. 'This is Mr Ashley who's come down from London because he's an expert on John Tamerton!' she finished a little breathlessly before seating herself in her grandmother's old chair, still unable to look at Edwin. P.C. Gibbons had opened a small notebook he carried, and, clearing his throat, began to read from it.

'West Devon Constabulary have come across a warehouse full of stolen property. There are several items which we know have come from recent burglaries in this part of the world. D.C. Ide thinks it could be worth your while going to have a look because there are several pictures there. Of course we don't know that they're yours, miss, but we'd be grateful if you'd clear the air one way or the other, so to speak.'

'Of course I'll go!' She sat up, her cheeks suddenly pink with colour. 'Oh! If only they were there...' She crossed her fingers; that would mean Edwin couldn't possibly be implicated, and that meant... But she wasn't brave enough to take that particular thought to its logical conclusion, although it was enough to send her off into one of her dreams.

'Miss Rivers?'

'Sue?' It took the combined efforts of both men to bring her back to earth, and this time she blushed in earnest.

'I'm so sorry,' she apologised. P.C. Gibbons stood up, his head just not touching the low beam that crossed the room.

'That's all right, miss!' He gave her a grin. 'I understand. I just hope that they are the right pictures after all.' He handed her a note with a phone number on it. 'Just give this number a call. They'll tell you how to get to it, and what time would be convenient!'

'It was really kind of you to call round and see me.'

'That's all right. It's on my way home... You won't go away again without letting me know, will you? I like to try and keep an eye open in my patch.'

'I certainly will!' she agreed fervently, following him out of the room. 'And I'm crossing my fingers that they are my pictures...'

'I'm sure you are. It's a crying shame someone had to do that to you, and your gran living here for I don't know how many years without any trouble.'

'It's a sign of the times, isn't it, Officer?' Edwin had come to stand next to her.

'I'm very much afraid so, sir. Today's cons know all about antiques and stuff like that. I heard that magazine *Country Life* is the favourite reading in the nick. They like to keep up on which manors have changed hands while they're inside!'

'I'm afraid its big business nowadays,' Edwin agreed. 'They'll fill a container and send it out to Australia, and bring one back in for good measure!'

'Australia, is it? Well, nothing would surprise me! I'll be on my way now, and you'll be in touch?'

'I'll call them and arrange a time tomorrow!' Sue agreed.

When she'd shut the front door, she turned to Edwin.

'Wouldn't it be marvellous if they were there?'

He smiled faintly as looked down into her eager face. 'Marvellous! But don't get your hopes too high, Sue. Will you let me drive you over tomorrow?' Once more her face flooded with colour. 'I promise to behave!' He gave her an outrageous smile. 'It'll be "look and don't touch", unless you'd like to continue where we left off?' One eyebrow rose in an enquiring quirk.

'No!' Her denial had an explosive quality about it, and he stepped back in mock-fear.

'OK, OK!' He raised both hands in mock-surrender. 'Do you want me to go away and find a pub to put me up for the night, or will you trust me yet again?'

Remember, a small voice spoke inside her, that he hasn't been proved innocent yet! 'I think you'd better understand that I'm not the sort of girl who sleeps around!'

He raised another enquiring brow at her, but she could see his mouth twitch with amusement.

'You're laughing at me!' she protested, a frown darkening her face.

'No, I'm not! Listen, you don't have to tell me that, I know!'

'How could you know?' She could have bitten her tongue out at this piece of imprudence on her part, but it was too late now, and he was laughing at her now, quite openly.

'My darling, it's written all over you! You've no need to spell it out. Anyone with a modicum of common sense could see the truth a mile away.'

'Then why are you laughing?'

'Because you look so outraged to be told that your virtue is so obvious!'

'You make me sound like some Victorian miss!'

His voice gentled. 'And why not? After all, you were brought up by one, weren't you?'

'Yes, well, Gran wasn't a namby-pamby little ninny, you know. She knew all about life!'

'I'm sure she did! It was quite a tribute to her that you came home quite willingly to live with her again, wasn't it?'

Sue bit her lip; really, this was becoming impossible. 'A tribute to my good nature, you mean!' He raised his brows a little, still questioning, and she flushed. 'Oh, all right, have it your own way! Yes, she was a remarkable person.'

'I've never doubted that. Now what's your answer? Are you going to turn me out, or can I stay here?'

Really there wasn't much of a tussle. If the truth were told she'd hated sleeping here alone, particularly in view of what had just happened.

'No, you can stay, Edwin, as long as you promise not to pounce!'

'I never pounce!' he teased. 'My technique is quite different...'

She stifled any desire on her part for him to enlarge on this interesting theme. 'Whatever,' she answered stiffly, 'I don't want to have to lock my door.'

'Sue!' He came to stand in front of her, his face quite serious. 'Surely you know I'd never do anything you don't like?'

'Yes, well, your idea of what I'm liking might not be quite the same as mine!'

His eyes narrowed in a teasing smile. 'Do you want me to put it to the test again?'

'No! And you can go to the pub if that's what you...'

He put a finger against her lips.

'Shh! Will you come out and have dinner with me this evening?'

'OK. But we'll have to hide the picture. I'm not leaving this house empty again to test providence! Someone might just have worked out by now that they've got a worthless copy instead of the genuine article, mightn't they?'

His eyes were serious. 'They might indeed!' he agreed.

He took her out to dinner where they both exerted themselves to find out as much as they could about each other. Edwin seemed to have decided to play it cool, maybe to lull her fears, she told herself scornfully; all the same she found him an entertaining companion, someone who was well travelled and well read and capable of being amusing without being spiteful about some of the more outrageous artistic luminaries of the day. She was curious to find out why he had decided to become such an expert on John Tamerton.

'You can blame my picture of your grandmother with the geese. It belonged to my uncle, and it always fascinated me, even when I was quite a young boy. I don't quite know why, I never have, unless it was precognition.'

Sue decided that avenue was better left unexplored, and enquired about his uncle.

'He was a charming old boy! I think you would have liked him, and he would certainly have liked you, because he too was inordinately fond of his little goose girl!'

She gave him a rather old-fashioned look, and once more changed the subject. 'Where on earth did you get your taste in clothes?' She'd met him outside the only bathroom in an outrageously joyful dressing-gown which had certainly raised her eyebrows. He laughed.

'My last girlfriend was an Italian, and she had very decided views on what she thought I ought to wear! Why? Would you rather I became the conventional upper-class Englishman like your ex, Justin?'

Her eyelids fluttered a little at this dig, but she refused to allow herself to be ruffled.

'No, not at all! I was just interested.' She gave him a sideways look. 'Most of them I know are far too conventional!'

'And you an ex-art student? I don't believe it!' he teased.

'Yes, they are! It's difficult to dress outrageously, if everyone does so. Anyway, most of them I knew were too poor to wear anything much except jeans, and their own painted T-shirts to liven things up, and perhaps the odd waistcoat!' She put her chin on her hands and began to laugh a little. 'I wonder if any of them will become works of art of the future? Chris, and he was really talented, used to paint original T-shirts to pay for his suppers at Gino's where we all used to eat because it was cheap!'

He laughed with her. 'It's an original thought, and reminds me of a Somerset Maugham short story I read once about how a famous artist in Paris tattooed some man's back and signed his work with his name. When the man had become old and poor, and the artist had become posthumously extremely famous, he sold himself for a comfortable old age to a gallery owner. Only he disappeared rather suddenly, and a rather unusual picture appeared in the gallery instead.'

'Ugh! That's sick! Are you trying to warn me against unscrupulous gallery owners?'

'Maybe!' he teased, then he took hold of her hand. 'You've nothing to fear from me, Sue. I want you to remember that!' He picked up his glass. 'Let's drink to a safe return of your pictures!'

'Yes!' At the thought of tomorrow her eyes sparkled.

Alone in her room, she lay in her bed trying to deny what heaven it would be if Edwin were there with her. She ought to be exhausted, but somehow she wasn't. How could anyone have felt her range of feelings for one man in so few hours?

She wanted to believe and trust him more than anything in the world, but because she had been hurt once before she was cagey about putting all her eggs in one basket. Already she accepted he had the power to hurt her as Justin never had, not even when she'd believed herself in love with him. Gran hadn't liked Justin the only time she'd met him, and she'd seen from Justin's face that he too had been rather horrified by the old woman, thinking of her as rather too plebeian to be the grandmother of his intended wife.

She'd noticed then that Justin kept on trying to dress up her background; concentrating on John Tamerton as if her more immediate relations weren't good enough. And now here was Edwin, who from his words was always going to find difficulty in reconciling her with the girl of his dreams. Georgina had been at pains to imply that she was not the sort of girl someone like him would wish to marry. That was so unfair, because she was not a promiscuous person at all. She'd been a virgin when Justin had eventually persuaded her into his bed, and had only agreed to sleep with him because she loved him so much.

How was she to compete with this image Edwin had inside his head? She wished with a passion that her grandmother were still alive, so that Edwin could understand that she was not and never could be the girl in the pictures; that just because she looked so like her, and even lived in the same sort of house, it did not mean that she could ever be a sweet Victorian innocent.

He'd woven a web of enchantment around them both this afternoon, and that was dangerous stuff. Real life was full of difficulties that meant one had to change and adapt. She didn't want to be Edwin's dream girl. She wanted to be loved in her own right, not just because she was the living embodiment of what seemed to be his love-affair with the whole Victorian artistic era.

CHAPTER SIX

'NO GOOD?' Edwin's compassionate face greeted her as she walked out of the barn-like building. Sue pinched her lips together, her disappointment easy to see, then shook her head. In truth she didn't trust herself to speak because after all Edwin had warned her not to let her expectations get too high as they'd driven over that morning.

He knew, she told herself furiously, that my pictures weren't there! Furious with him and even more so with herself, she got back into the car without having said a word. At least he had the good sense not to bother her with more false condolences. She brooded all the way home, sunk into the comfort of the leather seats, her mouth drooping sulkily, hardly hearing the classical music that Edwin was playing on a tape.

She wished she knew what to do next. She couldn't afford to have a row with him; not if she wanted to appear at his retrospective and give her little impromptu speech on Augustus Frome. That would make certain of putting the cat among the proverbial pigeons! And there'd be very little he could do about it except accept gratefully that she'd got the better of him!

She wondered too how long it would take him to work out that quite large parts of Gran's picture had been painted by a different hand. She had been very much the child of his old age, and John Tamerton's sight must already have been failing when she'd reached her early teens. Augustus Frome must have been a lifesaver for the older man in those latter years of his life before he admitted defeat. While she didn't doubt that the overall composition was her great-grandfather's work, much of the fine detail had been painted by Frome in her opinion.

Edwin had certainly told her nothing of his thoughts so far, but she could be patient. She just wished she could rid herself of that awful feeling she had that life wasn't really worth living any more. As the big car swept smoothly into the yard she roused herself sufficiently to check that there were no more outward signs of unwanted visitors.

She got out of the car, and, still suffering under a major sense of disillusionment, headed for the house, hardly caring what happened to Edwin.

He, after giving her departing back a frowning consideration, stayed seated in the car. It was painfully clear to him that she'd had a shock this morning; that in spite of his words of warning she'd pinned her hopes on finding her stolen property. In fact it seemed, despite what she'd said, that she still held him under suspicion, and that suspicion had hardened when she hadn't found her pictures.

He tapped one finger idly on the dashboard. He'd certainly tried to push her into a closer relationship than it seemed she was ready for, and yet he could have sworn she was not as indifferent to him as she pretended to be. Maybe it was time to teach her a little more forcefully that her destiny lay with him. He was too experienced a man not to know that her body responded to his with an enthusiasm that made his eyes glow in remembrance.

He found her in the kitchen, dispiritedly boiling a kettle to make them coffee. He waited until she finished, then sat down opposite her, his expression neutral in the extreme.

I'm behaving very badly! Sue told herself, but as she got a strange pleasure from doing so she'd no immediate intention of making the smallest effort to be nice to the monster who sat opposite her.

'Are you sure you don't want to change your mind about loaning me your grandmother's picture?'

Sue considered this to be an extremely sneaky attack on his part. Now she would be obliged to make an effort, or else all her plans over Augustus Frome would come to nothing.

'No, why should I?' She widened her eyes in mock-surprise, but had a nasty suspicion that she wasn't fooling the man sitting just a few feet away from her. 'You can take it back with you in your car if you like!'

Edwin looked momentarily shocked. 'Certainly not! With your permission, of course, I'll send down a specialist firm of removers. They'll make sure it's crated properly for the journey to London. Otherwise I think it had better stay hidden, don't you?'

'Perhaps that would be wise!' she agreed.

'Why not admit you're in a rage?' he attacked. Sue looked at him as if she could hardly believe her ears. 'I would be angry if I were you, and you look as if you're a cork about to explode out of a bottle!' The humorous understanding in his face didn't stop her from bursting into intemperate speech.

'We wasted the whole morning on a wild-goose chase going over to check some police haul near Tavistock. You even had the gall to warn me about not getting too excited! Well, let me tell you——' She broke off suddenly, and bit her lip savagely.

'I do hope you haven't been jumping to the wrong conclusions! I mean it's not as if there is any proof that I'm guilty, is there?' His ability to hit the nail right on the head made her cheeks flare in sudden burning colour. Surely she hadn't been that obvious?

'Why don't you admit you want to be involved with me? That's why you're in such a filthy temper, isn't it? You're at war with yourself!' Edwin's expression was reasonably non-committal, except for his eyes, which betrayed his inner amusement. How dared he behave so arrogantly? And he was still secretly laughing at her! Sue's eyes, now as cool and cold as any arctic glacier in a winter sea, met those warm brown ones.

'I don't know what you mean by "involved". Yes, you've tried to make love to me, but only, I think, because you wanted to see those pictures of my grandmother's. I wonder if I'd have rated very highly with you if it weren't for them?' she spat back at him. She wasn't going to forget in a hurry that he was known for having lots of gorgeous girlfriends. Why should she? The fact that he was sexy and had the power to disturb her dreams, as well as probably being responsible for stealing her pictures, just added to her misery.

'Why, you little horror!' Before she had any idea of his intentions, he'd moved quickly round the table and had picked her up in his arms. His lips found hers, and, powerless, she tried to twist her head away, but it was no good. His tongue probed deep into her mouth as she yielded to his particular touch; so skilful, so deliciously tormenting that her body betrayed her wilfully, delighting in his closeness. Later she didn't even want to fight him, and as if he was quite aware of it his grip on her loosened, as his hands began a sensual exploration of their own. Just for once she was going to revel in those feelings of security that being held in his arms gave her. She was selling out to the enemy, but somehow that didn't seem to matter at this particular moment.

She loved the clean, male smell of him, the way he could excite her just by being near her. That powerful male body was now exuding a burning heat and it seemed to her fanciful mind that all her millions of tiny little nerve-endings were responding, just as flowers did to the warmth of the sun. She was relaxing, opening up, as his lips gently explored her face and neck, seeking and finding those betraying pulses that told him her heartbeat had accelerated, his hands soothing and stroking her now tremblingly quiescent body.

'There, that's better, isn't it?' His voice sounded husky and low, and she was acutely aware of a satisfaction, as if he knew he had somehow conquered her enmity. Resentment bubbled up to pull her unwillingly out of his arms.

'Better for whom?' she queried, rudely, knowing her voice sounded betrayingly weak, but he didn't seem to mind her interjection. He watched the different expressions chase over her face, his own once more inscrutable, the light brown eyes hooded, as if unwilling to let her continue to read his inner self.

'I think I'd better leave after all...' he told her, his voice reflective. 'If I go now, I can be back in a couple of days. I don't think it's a good idea to leave you here alone for too long, particularly after what's just happened, do you?'

She tossed her head, determined not to admit anything else to him. He'd made her betray herself a little just now, but if he thought that little interlude was going to change anything between them then he'd have to think again! Just because she enjoyed his kisses it didn't mean she was prepared to give up her reservations about him; if anything her weakness paradoxically strengthened them.

'You don't need to worry about me, Edwin!' she told him proudly. 'This is my home.'

'All the same... is it possible that your housekeeper could at least come back to sleep here until I get back?'

She got cross. 'Edwin! You're not my minder!' She stamped her foot in her fury. Once more he flicked her a look that spoke volumes and fanned the flames of her temper.

'I am not behaving in a childish way!' she told him through gritted teeth. He raised his brows slightly.

'I didn't say you were,' he reminded her smoothly.

'No, but you looked it!' He smiled at her, a slow smile that helped to turn her bones to water.

'Here...' He reached behind him and picked up a bottle. 'May I give you a glass of your own wine?'

She gave him a sulky, brooding look but knew that if she wasn't to lose any more of her dignity she must smile and accept. 'Thank you...'

He poured himself a glass as well, and toasted her. 'You'd better believe I'll be back the day after tomorrow, Sue! It's no good protesting, and you ring your housekeeper and get her to come and sleep here with you. Promise?' Reluctantly she nodded, knowing she wouldn't feel happy alone at night, and that was one more thing to add to her feeling of resentment as far as he was concerned. He'd helped to destroy the peace of her home.

When he'd gone, having deliberately left his case and some of his things behind in the spare room, she was left feeling totally bereft. She could feel the tears welling up behind her eyes, and if she was going to cry then she preferred to do it in privacy without the possibility of being disturbed. Lying face down on her bed she knew she'd never felt so miserable in her life. Edwin had walked into her life and had taken it over in such a short time that she hardly knew how to accept or believe that such a thing could have happened to her.

Georgina's spiteful words at his party had hurt, and because of her previous experience with Justin she already half believed them. Also she was jealous. She knew Georgina found him attractive and that frightened her. Never before had she felt driven to snap at anyone as she had done to Edwin, and part of her was ashamed. When he was around she was in the grip of such overwhelming physical attraction that nothing else really seemed to matter. Her trying to drive him away today by her show of bad temper and frustration had been sheer perversity on her part. She'd done it deliberately because if she hadn't she knew she'd be at his mercy and he'd know it. Mind you, it had taken the wind out of her sails when he'd attacked her back...

She was using every feeble excuse in the book to deny that he was important to her, but, whether he was obsessed with her grandmother or not, she was in love with him. That was the painful truth which had to be faced and accepted. It didn't matter that they hadn't known each other very long; nothing mattered except the fact that they should be together always.

And suppose, that uncomfortable little internal voice asked, that he's only interested in an affair? What then? What indeed! Sue accepted that if he put up a determined assault she wouldn't be able to resist—indeed would most likely succumb with embarrassing speed in spite of Georgina's warning. So it became impossible for her to speak Edwin's name to anyone, even Bridget.

She was working rather dispiritedly alone in the studio the day he planned to return, when she heard the sound of his car. Her heart gave a great joyous leap before she sternly put it in its place, and she was half pleased when she was disturbed by the phone. Quite willing to be distracted, she picked it up.

'Hello?'

'Is that you, Sue?' She half recognised the voice, but couldn't put a name to it.

'It's Des. Listen, girl, I've found out something. Can I come and see you?'

'Found out something?' she echoed, trying to play for time.

'Yes!' His voice sounded impatient. 'Weren't you done over a week or so ago?'

'Yes. I lost some pictures...'

'Yeah, that's what I thought. I know where they've gone, girl!'

An arm snaked around her waist, and a kiss was pressed into her hair. She slanted Edwin a quick look but her concentration was almost totally on her conversation with Des. She swung away, putting up a warning hand to Edwin. He grinned at her, then walked back to his car to collect his luggage and bring it into the house.

'How do you know?' Her voice sounded sharp.

'Let's just say I've got me contacts in the business...' Something in his voice got to her, making her feel uncomfortable. She had a sudden quick vision of his long, rather thin nose.

'I'm sorry, Des, I'd rather you didn't come here. If you've got anything to say, then tell me now!'

'OK, girl, if that's the way you want it!' She heard the spite in his exaggerated drawl, and realised, rather belatedly, that once again she'd probably wounded his pride. 'I heard they're coming up in that sale in nineteenth-century art in Monte Carlo in a couple of weeks. Guess who had them sent out there? The Ashley Gallery!' She heard the sick glee in his voice and part of her wondered how on earth he knew that might hurt her. The phone was replaced at his end with a dull click and she was left standing in shock, the dialling tone buzzing its demand in her ear.

Like an automaton she replaced the receiver, but her legs felt trembly with shock, and she found she had to sit down rather hurriedly on the wood floor of the studio. To have your own worst fears confirmed was a disturbingly painful experience. She found she was talking to herself aloud, repeating over and over again, 'What shall I do? Oh, what shall I do?'

How long she stayed sitting she never knew afterwards, but it couldn't have been long, although she felt she'd aged a hundred years before she dragged herself wearily towards the kitchen and Edwin, and tried to plan what she had to do next. Would she be able to hide her distress from him? No, she couldn't, but if he could be brought to believe that it was shock, and only to do with hearing about her pictures being sold in France, then it might be all right.

It was impossible, even now, for her to consider involving the police. This was something she would have to do alone. If she took along the official description of her missing pictures, maybe the auctioneers would accept it. She certainly hoped so, because otherwise... But here her thoughts let her down. How could Edwin have been so confident, so stupid as to send her pictures to be sold under his gallery's name? But maybe he had been forced to because the auctioneers wouldn't accept anything of doubtful provenance.

She would have to go over to Monte Carlo and get the pictures withdrawn; what other choice did she have? It was something she must do alone, and in secret. No one must know of Edwin's involvement with her. Even now there was a sort of shock of disbelief that he had tried to cheat her and had so nearly succeeded. It took a very hardened criminal to have met her news with such innocent surprise. She remembered how she'd found it difficult to believe that he was behind the theft. At least Bridget wouldn't mind if she went away for a short break. It meant she'd be able to stay at home and not have to come and sleep in the small spare room every night.

Edwin came running lightly down the stairs but Sue's expression was still bleak and shocked as she took in how much he seemed at home.

'What was that all about?' He swung her around in his arms, his pleasure at seeing her again obvious. As his lips descended on hers, she closed her eyes to hide the incipient tears at the pain this crazy charade was giving her. 'Hey, what is it, sweetheart?' The endearment nearly finished her, and she pulled herself out of his circling arms.

'That was Des on the phone. He told me he thinks my pictures are due to come up in a sale in Monte Carlo in a couple of weeks.'

'What?' That one sharp word betrayed his interest. 'Is he sure?'

She shrugged her shoulders. 'He seemed pretty definite about it.'

He looked down at her, interest sharpening his features. 'I find that interesting...very interesting indeed.' He looked up quickly, too quickly for her to get her expression back under proper control. 'What are you planning to do about it?' The question was asked lightly, but she wasn't fooled for a minute.

'What can I do except go out there and see for myself?' she snapped back, goaded almost past control.

'I'm coming with you, then!'

'No!'

'Why not?' His eyes were hard with suspicion.

'Oh, I don't know!' Suddenly it became impossible to hide her tears. She sniffed unromantically, then turned away to pull off some kitchen roll to blow her nose.

'That doesn't look a nice hanky! Here, have mine...' A soft square of clean white cotton was pushed into her hand. Her fingers clutched it gratefully, and she wiped her eyes with it. It smelt a little of him, and she knew she wouldn't lightly return it.

'Why don't you go upstairs and wash your face while I get on and make the arrangements for us to fly to Monaco as soon as possible?'

Accepting the inevitable, and anyway longing to go up to her room and be alone, she left him.

'Well, what do you think?' Sue was already totally overwhelmed by sugar-icing architecture and the nymphs that appeared to be climbing every column, quite apart from the great chandeliers that dripped light. The Hotel de Paris was certainly living up to its great reputation. If it was a little outlandishly lush for her taste, it was also overpoweringly superb.

If Edwin wanted to take a suite, then good luck to him. He might think she was going to share it with him, but she had other plans! He had to be intent on making her final seduction a night to remember, because she guessed that the hotel's prices probably lived up to its exotic looks, and that would serve him right!

Once up in the suite, Sue looked around her with awe. A large drawing-room separated the two bedrooms, something that she viewed with satisfaction as she claimed the smaller of the rooms for her own.

Edwin took her in his arms, a teasing smile on his face. 'Still set on keeping me at a distance?'

She tried to push him away. 'Yes!' she answered tersely. 'This sort of thing...' she gave a wide sweep of her arm '...doesn't impress me at all!'

He gave a great shout of laughter. 'Oh, I already know that!'

She gave him a suspicious glance. 'How?'

'Because of the expressions on your face!' he teased. 'Anyway, you needn't be afraid I intend to seduce you, my little puritan...' He put one finger under her chin, tilting her face up.

'No?' she breathed.

He shook his head, his eyes laughing at her. 'No, not unless you want me to?'

A wave of colour flamed in her cheeks, shaming and embarrassing her, and his soft laughter didn't help. He knew her all too well, the rat! He thought all he had to do was kiss her into submission. Well, he was going to get a shock!

'I'm going to have a shower,' she told him, and marched firmly into the adjoining bathroom.

'OK... We'll meet later, shall we?'

Sue didn't answer, letting him think his question had been drowned in the noise of the water gushing fulsomely from the shower.

She waited what she hoped was a suitable length of time, then peeped out. She was alone. Quickly she grabbed her overnight bag and, with a wary eye on the other, now closed door of Edwin's room, quietly let herself out into the warm, early evening air.

'Miss Rivers?' The urbane gentleman who rose to greet her in a double-breasted navy blue pin-striped suit could have been from any European country. His English was spoken with barely any accent. He looked smooth, rich and faintly intimidating. 'I understand you have a problem which you think I may be able to help you with?' He sounded a little doubtful, as if he could think of no possible point of contact between them.

'I hope so, Monsieur d'Aussel. I understand you are offering for auction four unsigned pictures, probably by the English painter John Tamerton, in your next sale. I would be grateful if you would read these official police descriptions of the pictures to see if they match.'

Monsieur d'Aussel, looking as if there was a bad smell at the end of his nose, made no effort to take the papers from her hand. 'I can assure you, Miss Rivers, that there is absolutely no chance of our selling any work that is stolen. We are exceedingly careful. We check the source always, and if we are not satisfied then there can be no question of accepting anything from a doubtful background!' he finished proudly.

'I understand. No doubt you would accept paintings from the Ashley Gallery with little problem?'

'But absolutely! Of course Mr Edwin Ashley is an acquaintance of mine. We have done business together many times!'

'All the same I think if you look at these descriptions you will find that you are holding stolen paintings. In fact I must insist that you do so, otherwise I will be obliged to...'

The man sitting opposite her suddenly fixed her with an exceedingly shrewd eye, almost as if he was aware of her distress.

Monsieur d'Aussel stood up. 'Certainly, I will look now!' He flicked through the descriptions with surprising speed before handing them back to her. Was there a hint of compassion in his gaze? 'We do not want to bother the police, do we? These things are surely better sorted out with discretion, with tact... I think, *mademoiselle*, that perhaps you had better look at the pictures for yourself.'

Sue gave a shaky laugh. 'I think I had better, don't you?'

He wasted little time in conveying her through the large air-conditioned building which, to her untutored eye, appeared to be packed with treasures. 'The pictures are upstairs. Please follow me.' By this time Monsieur d'Aussel had been joined by his secretary and his assistant. Sue, intrigued in spite of herself, followed meekly past the massive racks stacked with pictures, some still being labelled with their lot numbers by a couple of porters who looked at their little party with curiosity.

Monsieur d'Aussel stopped in front of one rack. 'Miss Rivers, if you see anything you recognise, please let me know.'

It wasn't difficult. Her four unsigned pictures were there, but not her copy. Monsieur d'Aussel sighed as unhesitatingly she picked them out, then they began their return to his office, his rapid exchange in French with his assistant beyond her power to understand.

Alone with her once more in his office, he began to talk. 'You will realise, Miss Rivers, that I cannot take your word alone on this. Perhaps you will give me some telephone numbers so I may check?'

'Of course. Here is my solicitor, also the local police who dealt with the burglary.'

'Thank you.' He stood up. 'We hope not to keep you waiting too long. This is very unfortunate, very unfortunate indeed! We have your hotel number? No? You'll call me? I see!' He shook her hand. 'May I hope that in spite of this unpleasantness you will enjoy your time in Monaco?' He gave her a quick, professional smile. 'Until we meet again, yes?'

Turned loose once more into Monte Carlo's narrow streets, she wandered rather aimlessly downhill until she came to the port. In spite of the hard times with recession that had bothered most of Europe, there seemed little sign of it here. Large sailing yachts, motor cruisers of startling size and opulence lay cheek by jowl in the shimmering blue waters of the Mediterranean. The musical clatter of the rigging in the light breeze drew her nearer, as she slowly walked past these monuments to a taste that she found fascinating yet slightly obscene in its extreme luxury.

She spent the rest of the day wandering aimlessly around the principality, terrified that Edwin would somehow find her, yet enjoying the occasional sugar-pink glimpses of the castle that was home to the

Grimaldi family, admiring the grand façade of the casino, and wondering whether she dared go there that evening. But all the time she was conscious of an ache inside that wouldn't go away. In spite of her efforts it was impossible to hide her sadness at what she had to accept. She'd fallen in love with a thief, one who'd stolen her heart as well as her pictures, and because of that she was incapable of handing him over to the police.

She wondered how Des could possibly have known that those pictures were hers, unless he'd heard Edwin discussing them; indeed for all she knew it could have been Des who'd been given the job of removing them from the studio, and been told to look out for the girl with the goats. After all, it had been Des who'd first told her about Edwin...

She returned to the small hotel she'd found on her own, tired, as well as hot and sticky, and more than looking forward to a shower.

'Sue?'

She looked up in disbelief to see Edwin's concerned face. As he came closer, his image began to shiver then break up in a haze of light. The last thing she remembered was feeling unpleasantly sick and dizzy before she blacked out.

She came round uncertain where she was. There was a murmur of voices, then the sound of something being poured... She opened her eyes.

'Ah, you've come round, have you?' She looked up into worried brown eyes. '*Madame* said you would. She also said this tisane would make you feel better.'

Sue had been conscious for some time of a slightly odd sort of herby smell around her. She tried to sit up, her memory returning, aware that she must look a complete mess.

'Take it slowly! You might faint again.' She was aware of a strong arm, and as she still felt slightly swimmy in the head she was grateful for its support. 'Here, try a sip of this...' The smell became stronger as the cup was held close to her mouth. Weakly, she grasped it with both hands and took a sip. It didn't taste particularly nice, but then on the other hand it wasn't nasty. She sipped again without enthusiasm.

'Something tells me that you'd trade that for a good cup of tea or coffee!'

Quite unable to meet his eyes, she gave a small smile. 'You couldn't be more right!'

'Well, which is it to be? Tea or coffee? Unless you're prepared to drink your tea without milk I'd recommend the coffee because you won't like the taste of the milk!'

'I've already discovered that! But tea without milk, please...'

'Right!' He got up and left the room, leaving Sue free to make her rather wobbly way towards the tiny *en-suite* bathroom. Horrified by what she saw in the mirror, she locked the door, and turned on the shower before undressing.

Feeling much refreshed, she came out later wrapped in a towelling robe to find Edwin sitting out on the small balcony that looked over the red rooftops with the occasional distant view of the sea. On the table by the bed was a tea-tray and without wasting any more time she sat down and poured herself a cup, putting in a thin slice of lemon. She was just finishing her second cup when she was aware that Edwin had come in and was now leaning against the sliding window, watching her.

Although it was maddening, she couldn't stop the wave of colour that washed over her face, although her eyes remained wary.

'Feeling better?' he enquired, and she nodded, carefully replacing the cup on the tray in case the inner tremors that shook her became too obvious.

'It isn't difficult to guess what you're thinking! I suppose that was why you ran out on me last night?'

Her eyes met his then, and she got a shock. He was furious. *He* was furious? The weak and trembly part of her subsided as her own anger rose to meet his. What right had *he* got to be angry? He ought to be on his bended knee, thanking her for not betraying him to the police. He ought... With difficulty she tried to control her unruly thoughts.

'I find you, on the other hand, rather more difficult to fathom!' The grey eyes filled with righteous indignation as she challenged him.

'If you hadn't just passed out on me, I'd be tempted to put you over my knee and do what your father ought to have done when you were a child!'

Sue could hardly believe her ears. This was unreal, surreal... 'Have you gone quite mad?' she gasped, unable for the moment to think of anything else more suitably crushing. He raised his eyebrows and let a small silence grow between them so that she would be more than aware what he thought of her last question.

'Why didn't you tell me that you knew your pictures had been sent out here by the Ashley Gallery?' he asked in a voice that sounded so reasonable that she was left gaping at him like an idiot with her mouth half open.

'Why didn't I...? You *must* be mad! Let you know I've discovered you're behind their sale?'

'It would have been the most sensible thing to do, and, if you'd bothered to think it out in an sensible manner, that's what you would have done!'

Sue opened her mouth, then shut it again, by now totally at a loss for words. He watched her, a sardonic expression on his face, as he leant against the sliding glass door. Today he was wearing a charcoal-grey suit with a plain light blue shirt and a tie. Conventional, with black Gucci-type loafers on his feet, he was every inch the professional businessman. With massive self-restraint, she continued.

'You think I, having been told that your gallery had sent my stolen pictures to France to be sold, should have told you what I'd found out? I've heard of brazen effrontery, but I never thought I'd ever have to justify it face to face!'

'Why don't you use that brain of yours? Didn't it cross your mind that, always supposing I was a thief, it was strange I should have sent stolen goods to be sold quite openly under my own name? That as I'm the acknowledged expert on John Tamerton it was inevitable I'd be asked to verify the fact that they are genuine by at least one buyer of these pictures? That the description of these pictures is already circulating, via Interpol, the art dealers of Europe?'

He gave her a quick glance. 'Of course you may think all dealers are crooks! But I can assure you that there are some honest ones among us, and if you hadn't come charging over here, blackening my name——'

'Blackening your name?' Sue interrupted, furiously. 'I went to extreme lengths not to involve you with the police, which I could have done! Oh, yes, I could have done! Anyway, how dare you accuse me of blackening your name? Nine people out of ten——'

'Would have sat down and thought out the whole thing logically, instead of jumping to the wrong conclusions!'

'Oh? Would they?' Sue crossed her arms over her chest. 'Why don't you tell me who did send my pictures over here to be sold, then?'

'I don't know. Yet.' He looked all at once cold, like a stranger.

'You *don't know*,' she mimicked, 'yet I'm supposed to guess who isn't guilty! Well, let me tell you, Edwin Ashley, that I don't have that sixth sense either! I just worked on a strong probability that as you owned the Ashley Gallery you'd know how my pictures have turned up in Monaco!'

Edwin was looking at her with an extremely thoughtful expression on his face. 'I suppose there's no chance that those French cousins of yours could be involved?'

'Hardly.' She gave him a thin smile. 'You see, you're really the only person who knew about those pictures, apart from Bridget. Oh, my cousins might have known about them in theory, but I can't see them bothering with them, not when they knew about the other—the girl with the goats! I was going to ask you where my copy of that has gone. You see, I wondered if someone had bothered to get in touch with my cousins thinking it's genuine. They'd give a great deal to get their hands on that, of course, but they know about my copy.' She gave him a straight look. 'It gets rather awkward, doesn't it? The field is rather narrow, unless you discussed my pictures with anyone else?'

'You'll have to take my word that I haven't discussed your affairs with anyone.' Again he answered in that light, dangerous voice of his.

'But suppose I don't believe you? You know, I got the impression that time I met her at your gallery that your assistant, Georgina, knew Des... I wonder if you told her about my pictures?'

'That's enough, Sue! Until I have proof I'm not accusing anyone.'

'Really? You've already accused me of behaving like an idiot!'

'That rankled, did it? Well, so it should! You should have told me! And if you weren't so pigheaded and obstinate you'd have done so! Even if you thought I was the thief, you must have known that once you knew about the sale the pictures were safe. God knows what Monsieur d'Aussel thinks of it all.'

Provoked beyond all reason, Sue stood up. 'Who cares what Monsieur d'Aussel thinks? I don't!' she shouted.

'Then you should!' Just for a moment Edwin smiled. 'A large part of my business is based on Europe. If I lose his good opinion, think of the money I stand to lose if he doesn't trust me any more!'

'I couldn't care less!' Poor Sue was scarlet in the face with rage and mortification. Loud knocking on the door momentarily distracted her.

'Yes? I mean, *entrez.*' *Madame* from behind the desk peered rather coyly around the door, then addressed a question in rapid French to Edwin which was quite beyond her.

'What is she saying?' Still furious, Sue stamped her foot.

'*Oh, mon Dieu!*' With a roguish look, and another quick burst of French, *madame* shut the door, leaving them alone together.

'Tell me, Edwin, what did she want?'

'She wanted to know if you were all right. I told her you were fine, and she said she could see that, and she hoped we'd make up our quarrel very soon!'

'That's none of her business! Anyway, she shouldn't have let you into my room. Why, you might have been a...a...' She hesitated, which was fatal as Edwin interrupted.

'I told her you were my fiancée!' he answered smoothly.

'You told her what?' she screeched.

'Shh!' Edwin held up his hand. 'Do you want her to come back?'

'No! I want you to get out of my room, now!' She marched over to the door and held it open. 'Get out, Edwin! And don't you dare come near me again until you've apologised, and returned my pictures!'

'OK.' He unfolded his arms and walked towards the door. 'Don't be too hasty when you hear a knock on the door in a minute or two. It'll be *madame* with something for you to eat. She told me you were cross because your blood sugar was low!' He gave her a rather sarcastic smile as he walked through the door, and Sue slammed it shut on him in a fury.

The low-down, two-faced toad! He was arrogant, infuriating, and he had no right to come meddling in her affairs without her express invitation! Was he grateful that she'd managed to locate all but one of her pictures? No, he was not! He'd even had the audacity to give her a lecture on the subject. If he wasn't responsible for the theft of her pictures then it had to be somebody close to him, didn't it? Who better than Georgina, whom she'd disliked on sight?

Now this was a happy turn of thought. If he wasn't responsible for the theft ... She went back to sit down on the bed, absent-mindedly pouring herself another cup of tea. So, it was lukewarm, but did she care? Not Sue! Not now she was beginning to be convinced that Edwin hadn't anything to do with the theft of her pictures. Georgina. What possible reason could she have for doing something so crazy? If she was found out she'd lose her job... Sue knitted her brows. It didn't make sense. And if it was Des who'd done the dirty, then why ring her up to tell her? She shook her head, which was beginning to swim again.

When *madame* came in with a tray containing a delicious little omelette and salad, and a small pot of caramelised custard, Sue realised that she really was very hungry indeed. It was difficult even to remember that she was cross with her for allowing Edwin into her room. *Madame* laid the tray down on the small table by the window, talking all the time. Sue, understanding only about one word in every six, was reduced to smiling, but as she sat down and smelt the omelette she was quite unable to stop herself breaking a small piece of bread with rather too much eagerness to be ladylike, so it was rather an apologetic smile she gave *madame* as the woman left the room saying, '*Bon appetit!*'

All the same, even after she'd eaten and was rested, she still couldn't unravel the puzzle in front of her. She couldn't seem to fit the separate pieces together so that they made sense. She was half dozing when she was disturbed by the shrill demand of the phone.

'Sue? It's Edwin. Monsieur d'Aussel and I have managed to sort out your pictures for you. I've arranged for them to be returned to you, probably by some time next week if that's all right?' He didn't wait for her acknowledgement. 'By the way, are you feeling better?'

'Yes.' She couldn't stop her voice sounding stiff. He laughed.

'Good! Maybe that'll teach you not to wander around Monte Carlo without stopping for lunch.'

'How do you know I spent the day walking?' she demanded involuntarily.

'It wasn't very difficult to guess. You looked very tired before you literally fell at my feet!' He waited a little, just to see if she was to be tempted into speech, but Sue had already decided to keep quiet before her unruly tongue could get her into any more trouble.

'I wondered if you'd spend the evening with me. I mean, here we are, both alone. It seems a pity we should be condemned to solitary dinners. If you agree I had sort of planned a dinner for two, then perhaps we could visit the casino, just to see if we feel like breaking the bank. After all, we have something to celebrate, don't we?'

'I suppose so...' But she wasn't capable of keeping the smile out of her voice. 'Mind you, the way you were talking to me earlier deserves an apology, don't you think?'

'I'll apologise to you if you'll apologise to me for thinking I was a thief! Agreed?'

She giggled. 'OK. But you've got to bring me proof you're innocent!'

'No problem! You sound a little happier, by the way. Was the omelette good?'

'Absolutely delicious. And the pudding was even better!'

'Good. So we don't need to eat too early, then. I'll come and pick you up at nine. OK?'

'OK.' She put the phone down carefully, then got up and did pirouettes around the room. If anyone had told her this morning that she was going to have fun in Monte Carlo she'd have laughed in their face, but now! She stopped and smiled at herself in the mirror. It was a good thing she'd brought one smart dress with her, wasn't it?

CHAPTER SEVEN

SUE took a last look at herself in the mirror and was satisfied. The sleeveless blue shirt dress was long, midcalf and buttoned the whole way through; a pure line which allowed a long glimpse of leg. White calf sandals, slightly platformed, added a good half-inch to her height. She looked serene yet elegant, in fact exactly how she wanted to look. She held up some large pearl beads to see if they would look good around her neck, then shook her head; they would spoil the simplicity of the whole look, so, wearing no jewellery at all, she went down to find Edwin.

Both he and *madame* greeted her with flattering approval. Edwin's eyes gave her a comprehensive and detailed study, yet there seemed to be a shade of reserve in his expression, which slightly worried her.

'I like the dress!' he smiled, but she was sure with a little constraint in his manner. She raised her eyebrows a little then smiled back, but there was an unspoken query in her look which ensured her reply would be brief and to the point.

'Good.' She slung a woven black and white cotton chenille cardigan jacket over her shoulders as he politely held the door open for her.

'I thought we'd go and eat at Rampoldi's, unless you fancy Italian cooking tonight?'

'Anywhere, I don't mind, but I warn you now that I'm feeling hungry again!' She tried with a show of laughing enthusiasm to put the fun and, more importantly, her anticipation of greater things to come back in their togetherness, but without success it seemed. Edwin appeared content to keep his distance.

'Here...' He opened the door of a waiting taxi, and Sue, whose feet and leg muscles were still a bit sore after her walking all day, was grateful. She smiled to herself as she saw him watch the inevitable leg show while she got into the taxi, but then what woman really minded being appreciated by a man? He joined her, saying, 'I thought you'd be tired if you've been on your feet all day.'

'I'm not exactly tired, but I have to admit I'm conscious that I've walked too far today!'

'That's what I thought,' he agreed, a touch formally, and Sue gave up. Whatever it was that had put a damper between now and their last meeting was obviously important enough for him to ignore her signals that her guard, as far as he was concerned, was now totally down.

Rampoldi's was just behind the casino, within easy walking distance in fact, and facing the casino gardens. Maybe she was being over-sensitive, but his extreme good manners smacked somehow of dismissal, and this heightened her colour. On the surface he could hardly have appeared more considerate for her comfort, but underneath she was aware that she was being treated with a reserve, almost as if he'd heard something to her discredit.

Dinner was long and leisurely with both of them appearing to enjoy the unaccustomed warmth of the night air as well as the cooking. For all her vaunted hunger, though, Sue found she couldn't eat a great deal because she was far too aware of the dark man who sat so close to her. She allowed her eyes to become riveted to little things about him, like the dark hairs on his wrist beneath the gold Rolex and the absurd length of his eyelashes. When he smiled one side of his face creased into a dimple. She found herself longing to touch it delicately with one finger.

The tension between them had become almost palpable by its intensity, both of them so aware of each other that they communicated that awareness to others around them. Even his breath on the bare skin of her arms was capable of raising goose-pimples. Suddenly she could bear it no longer. Whatever had gone wrong must be brought out into the open between them.

'What is it, Edwin?' Her grey eyes, candid and beautiful, met his brown ones. He didn't pretend to misunderstand her.

'I spoke to Des on the phone this evening!' His voice sounded blunt, almost brutal in its flat tones.

'Yes?' she said. He looked with astonishment at her eager face. 'Did he tell you how he found out about the pictures?' His dark brows drew together in a frown. 'Well, go on, don't keep me in suspense!' Sue knew she ought to feel sorry that he was going to have to admit Georgina's treachery to her, but she couldn't pretend any longer.

'He told me the whole thing had been set up by you as part of a scheme to discredit my name!' he finished harshly.

Sue sat back in her chair, an expression of thunderstruck amazement on her face. 'He said what?' She shook her head in disbelief, then looked at him, her glance becoming accusing. 'And you believe him?' she asked in an appalled whisper.

He looked uncomfortable. 'Why should he lie?'

'God knows! Although I suppose I could make an educated guess as to who put him up to it! Anyway, why should I be interested in discrediting your name?'

Once more he looked uncomfortable, then gave a small shrug of his shoulders. 'I've been told that ever since your affair with Justin Poole went wrong you've had a chip on your shoulder about not being quite good enough for someone of his background. That, in short, you've become rather involved in feminist issues, and would enjoy putting me down over the question of Augustus Frome...'

Once more Sue looked at him with utter astonishment. 'Now don't tell me you heard all that from Des?' she enquired, a shade sarcastically. A dull flush warmed his skin. 'I see! That convenient little version of events came from your assistant, did it?' She gave him a look of scorn. 'You needn't bother to answer—the truth is written all over your face!' She stood up, and he did the same, so that they faced each other like warriors of old, their sudden, mutual antagonism for each other thinly veiled.

'You haven't denied it!' he accused, to be met with a look of pitying contempt.

'Why should I bother to deny something that's such an obvious load of rubbish that only a credulous fool could possibly believe it?' Two spots of colour burned fiercely on her cheeks, as her voice got higher and louder.

'What do you expect me to believe? That both Des and Georgina are lying, while you're telling the truth?'

She didn't miss the sarcasm behind his thinly disguised belief that two against one proved him right.

'Why not? Or is Miss Foliot so grand that she's above the need to lie?' Allowing her jealousy of Georgina to get an upper hand proved to be a mistake.

'So you do hold a grudge against her and her family!'

'Hold a grudge against her family? I don't even know them! And if she's anything to go by then I haven't missed much!' she answered furiously.

'*Monsieur, mademoiselle!*' The head waiter was standing by their table pleading with them. All eyes on the surrounding tables were turned in their direction, but they ignored him.

'I think you've just proved my point, haven't you? Your irrational dislike of Georgina, whom you hardly know...'

'Thank God!' Sue interjected.

'...just confirms what she told me about you!'

Sue leant forward, resting both hands on the table. 'Before you go on jumping to conclusions, Edwin Ashley, I'd just check that your *assistant*——' she spat the word out '——doesn't turn out to be an old acquaintance of that little rat Des! I know you had to have told Georgina about my pictures, because how else would they have known how to cook up this little ploy? Justin warned me that Georgina considers you to be her property, and that she was the sort of girl who'd go to extreme lengths to get her way.' She gave him a tight little smile. 'I wish you luck with her! Any girl prepared to go to these lengths just to keep on the right side of her boss...'

She shook her head at him. 'How can you be so blind? When I think just a few hours ago how pleased I was to discover that you weren't the thief after all! Whereas now...' She swung away in disgust, then, pushing aside the agitated head waiter, stalked out into the night, tears pouring down her face, ignoring a cry from Edwin to come back. She knew the waiter would make sure he didn't leave without paying his bill, and she intended to be away before he could come and find her.

She hailed a taxi to take her to her hotel. Commanding the driver to wait, she went up to her room and hurriedly packed. She settled her account with the night porter, and then, grateful to be spared *madame*'s attention, ordered the taxi to take her to Nice Airport. Just after they left, she noticed another taxi pull up at the hotel, and though she couldn't swear to it she thought the man who got out was Edwin. A fierce pain in her heart warned her that she had been wise to run. There had to be some flight she could catch, particularly when she didn't much care what her final destination was!

She got home the following day, having spent a miserable night outside Paris in an airport hotel. She was greeted by Bridget, whose worried look disappeared at the sight of her.

'Where have you been? And what *have* you been doing? I've had the police round, who informed me your pictures have been found in Monaco of all places! Your solicitor wants to talk to you, and last, but not least, Edwin Ashley has been ringing just about every half-hour to find out if you're home!'

Sue dropped her bag on to the kitchen floor. 'I've been in Monaco, of course!'

Bridget's jaw dropped. 'But you never warned me you were going abroad!'

Sue sighed. 'Sit down and I'll tell you all about it!'

The phone started to ring, and Bridget automatically got to her feet, before subsiding again.

'Sorry! It's bound to be for you.'

'No, you answer it. And if it's Edwin Ashley, don't tell him I'm home!'

'But why not?' Bridget looked bewildered. 'I thought you were mad about him!'

'I'll tell you in a minute. Now do go and answer it!' She listened to Bridget's one-sided conversation, full of such choking pain that she felt quite faint. Why couldn't he leave her alone? Or perhaps he'd already warned the police that she was responsible for the theft of her own pictures? She buried her face in her hands. What was she to do?

Bridget's return to the table had her wearily sitting up. 'You look awful, dear!' Bridget exclaimed. 'And why all this pretending to be Garbo?'

It hurt to speak about what had happened, but Sue did, sparing herself nothing.

'So you see, he believes Georgina and Des. I suppose it's hardly surprising, two against one, you know!' she finished. Bridget looked absolutely horrified.

'I can't believe it. What a nasty piece of work that girl must be!'

Sue shrugged. 'Yes, but what can I do about it? Nothing! Edwin obviously finds it impossible to believe she'd do such a thing... To be fair, from his point of view I must have sounded just as unbalanced as Georgina made me out to be!'

Bridget was silent for a moment, then commented, 'From what you've told me it must have been quite a row.'

Sue gave her a faint smile. 'It was! And a very public one at that!'

'Why do you suppose Des lied to Edwin in the first place? I mean, he doesn't strike me as someone, from all you've told me about him, who'd do something like that unless it was made worth his while.'

'Oh, I don't know! He was a bit peeved I wasn't prepared to let him come and see me here, and he didn't like me giving him the brush-off earlier. I think I wounded his pride...'

'Well, if he knows that assistant, that Georgina, I should think she's given it a dent or two by now, wouldn't you think?'

'Well, they're certainly two of the most unlikely allies... You know, when I'd recovered from passing out at Edwin's feet, and he'd been ticking me off for not telling him Des had told me that the Ashley Gallery had sent my pictures to Monaco, I was so happy... You see, I'd been so frightened, and more than half convinced that he was behind it all, that it was the most tremendous relief to discover that he had to be innocent after all. When he rang later that afternoon to fix a date, I was over the moon. Oh, I know I should have been on my guard, but——' she half shrugged '—it was too late! I had my doubts whether it was me he was really interested in, or some kind of image of the past... I suppose I still don't know, but even that hasn't really made any difference to my feelings for him.' She sighed.

'You look absolutely exhausted, dear—why don't you go to bed? You need to rest!' Bridget took charge, as she so often had in the past when Sue was a child, and Sue sniffed, trying to control her tears.

Much later on, tucked up in her bed and feeling a great deal better from having eaten a light supper and having Bridget's comforting presence to draw on, she was able to ask her the one important, burning question.

'Bridget, what shall I do about Edwin?'

'I don't think there's a lot you can do, dear, except leave it to him. By the way he's been behaving on the phone, I'd say he was pretty much regretting that row you had. I mean he's obviously worried stiff about you!'

'Serve him right!' Sue's mouth drooped in a sulky line. 'He deserves to be worried after what he accused me of!'

Bridget gave her a kind smile. 'Don't forget you too had grave suspicions about his honesty!' she reminded her. 'He's not a fool. He must have known in part what you were thinking!'

But this didn't suit Sue at all, and she hunched her shoulders in negation. 'Nobody else but you and he knew about the pictures, so unless he discussed it with Georgina who else could there be?'

'Your cousins? You know, if I were you I think I'd at least try to make quite sure they aren't involved. I mean, it would be pretty embarrassing to discover that they were at the bottom of it all the time, wouldn't it?'

'Yes, but I don't see how they can be, do you?' Sue sat up in the bed and hugged her knees.

'Oh, I don't know... Suppose they'd paid Des to check up on you. What then?'

Sue slid her eyes sideways to look at her friend. 'That would be a bit of a long shot, if not stretching coincidence too far!'

'I don't know.' Bridget looked quite animated, obviously enjoying every minute of the drama. 'Where do your cousins live?'

'Well, they have the *mas* in Provence, but I think they're both based in Paris where they work.'

'There you are, then! You should go and see them.'

Sue shut her eyes. 'Have a heart! I've just got back from Paris today. I'm not going to go back there and waste my money on some wild-goose chase.'

'Well, you could at least call them and try to find out if someone has offered them your copy of the goose girl!'

'You know, that's not a bad idea. Anyway, I want that picture back!' She looked at her clock. 'It's not too late. I'll call their apartment now!'

She went downstairs to the phone, found the number, and dialled.

'Céci, hi! It's Susan. Yes. How are you? Good, and Michel? Fine. Look, I'm sorry to call you this late but I wondered if you have been offered Gran's picture with the goats? You have? That's great!' She was silent for quite a long time, Bridget listening impatiently to the barely audible quacking of the distant voice.

'Yes, it is my copy. What? Oh, you guessed it probably was? You were going to get in touch? Listen, it was stolen, along with those four unsigned pictures from here... Don't worry, I've got the others back; they were in Monaco! No! They're OK, yes... So, what about my picture? They want you to come to London!' Her eyes looked up to meet Bridget's in a blaze of light. 'You will now agree to come? That's great! What's that? They want to meet in your hotel room next Wednesday? Around six-thirty? Fantastic! I'll be there waiting for them... Yes... I'll be in touch. No, and Céci? Thanks very much and congratulations!' She put down the receiver carefully, then looked up with a smile.

'You were right! They were offered the picture by an Englishman last week. At first she was a bit sticky—she's just got engaged and she wasn't really interested, neither was Michel, because they guessed it was probably only my copy. Anyway, she's going to agree to come over. I've got to book a room in her name in a hotel, then I can wait and see just who turns up with it!'

Bridget smiled with pleasure, then her brow puckered, and she shook her head.

'No, that isn't going to work, my dear! You've got to have Edwin there with you. He'll never believe you if he doesn't see this happen with his own eyes.'

'Edwin? Oh, Bridget, I can't!'

'Then you must call the police! Look, you can't hide from Edwin forever, not with all that unfinished business between you. Anyway, what could be more logical? You've contacted your cousins and they've confirmed they've been offered your copy... I must say I wonder why they weren't offered the other pictures as well.'

'I think whoever it was that took them realised that they could be too valuable; that my cousins would probably check up with me. Anyway, it was always intended, I think, that they should be found before they were sold.'

'Then why try to sell your copy?'

'I think that could be a touch of spite on someone's part. Firstly because it isn't what they hoped it was, and secondly because it was painted by me.'

'You certainly can't wait in that hotel room all alone!'

Sue gave a sigh. 'No, I suppose you're right. I'll have to get in touch with Edwin.' But Bridget noticed with satisfaction that her mouth trembled as she said his name.

'I'll call him tomorrow evening. There's no point in talking to him at the gallery—Georgina might overhear something...' Sue stopped suddenly. 'Oh, lord! Do you think he'll tell her about it?'

'Not if you tell him not to, and make it sound important enough!'

Sue didn't answer, but from the expression on her face Bridget knew she had escaped once more into her dreams. At least this time they looked as if they might be pleasant ones; that she had somehow escaped from her unhappiness momentarily. As she got up to leave the room she told herself that the path of true love never did run smooth, and that it was a good thing that Sue looked like getting married at last, because she backed Edwin's steely determination to triumph over her hurt feelings and wounded heart. Whatever he might have said to her in the heat of the moment Bridget hoped that he was as hooked on her as Sue was on him. He'd sounded steadily more distraught as the hours had gone by with no news of Sue's return.

In fact as Edwin rang before eight o'clock the following morning and Sue happened to be nearest the phone, she answered it.

'Sue? You're home, then?'

It didn't help that her whole body seemed to come alive when she heard his voice. Furious at the great leap her heart gave, she had no difficulty in sounding sulky. 'It's a bit early to call, isn't it? It's only just after half-past seven!' she answered ungraciously.

'I'm sorry I woke you up. I suppose you got home late last night?'

'No, not that late...' She debated whether to tell him the truth, then decided against it. There wasn't much point in making him mad if she wanted his co-operation next week. 'Edwin? Look, I've managed to discover something. I was talking to my cousin Cécile and she told me that someone has offered her my copy of the goat girl. The plan is for the seller to meet her in a hotel room next Wednesday at about six-thirty in the evening. I've arranged to take her place, and I think it would be a good idea if you came too.'

'Is that where you were? Did you go to see your cousins when you left Monaco?'

She was pleased to hear the concern in his voice. 'Not exactly; anyway, it doesn't matter. Will you agree to be with me when this man brings my picture to the hotel?'

'Of course I will!' She heard the hint of impatience in his voice. 'But are you sure you can trust your cousin over this? I understood there was bad blood between you.'

'I think it's OK now. Céci has just got engaged to be married, and Michel, guessing it was only my copy, isn't interested. No, she won't cause any trouble. She was rather shocked to hear about the burglary.'

'Well, I can understand that; after all she's not the only one, is she? It's caused both of us a great deal of unnecessary trouble!' Sue heard the flat sincerity in his voice with a sinking heart. So, he was still angry, was he?

'I'm hoping that whoever comes to the hotel with my picture will at least be able to unravel some of this tangle!' she answered bitterly.

'Let me book the hotel, will you?'

'I'm not sure that would be wise, Edwin. I hope by the way that you won't mention this to anyone at all. In fact I'd prefer to have your promise over that!'

'I can assure you I can keep a discreet tongue in my mouth,' he answered stiffly. 'You needn't worry that Georgina will know anything about it!'

'Good! But as my cousin always stays in the same hotel when she comes to London I think it would be easier if I booked the room.'

'As you wish! I take it you'll let me know nearer the time which one I'm supposed to meet you at?'

So now he was offended, was he? Well, it wouldn't hurt him after everything she'd had to suffer from him.

'Don't worry, I'll be in touch. It would be better if I called you at your flat, wouldn't it? I don't want to chance my luck. Georgina might not let me talk to you if she recognised my voice.'

He heard the bitterness in her voice and gave an exaggerated sigh. 'I wish you'd stop being so stupid about her! She's far too adult to have got herself mixed up in an affair like this.'

There was a nasty silence. Then, 'Gran always said there was none so blind as those who won't see!' she shouted. Furious, she banged the phone down. It was far too early in the morning for dramatics; anyway, she might seriously have lost her temper again with him. Why couldn't he see that Georgina was as predatory as any tiger stalking its prey? And yet she would never have put him down as a stupid man by any means. Georgina must have been very clever if he really didn't have a clue that she was after him, and Sue found that thought profoundly depressing. Edwin's unwillingness to believe that his assistant could possibly be mixed up in this possessed her mind to an alarming extent. Unless Georgina could be caught, red-handed, Edwin might never believe her to be totally innocent, however much he wanted to.

The Knightsbridge Park Hotel, solid, old-fashioned in outward appearance, was large enough to offer a certain amount of anonymity. It was a good hotel without being quite in the class of the Ritz, yet offered slightly old-fashioned comfort with large rooms and *en-suite* bathrooms still marble-tiled and with their original plumbing. Sue had distant memories of staying here with her father and grandmother on their infrequent trips to London. In a way it was rather homely with its distant familiarity, its solid red carpets and great staircase that led out of the hall to a half-landing with shops and the big sitting-room that looked out on to the park.

She had booked and paid for the room in her cousin's name, in fact using it herself the night before. She put far too much importance on this meeting to leave anything to chance, so she had come up the evening before, and if staying in the hotel left a considerable hole in her finances, well, she hoped it was all going to be worthwhile. After all, what price could be put on her whole future happiness?

Mademoiselle Cécile Tamerton was staying in the hotel her family had always used on their visits to England. She had left instructions at the desk that anyone asking for her was to be given her room number; that she was expecting a couple of visitors, one of whom maybe would have a picture with him. She was also very careful to keep herself hidden. She knew her distinctive platinum-blonde hair could be recognised at a distance, so she had been a virtual prisoner in her room all day.

Edwin arrived early, and after taking one look at her strained face picked up the phone to call Room Service. He ordered a bottle of champagne to be delivered to her room and some smoked salmon sandwiches. This made Sue furious.

'I hope you're going to pay for it!' she spat. 'Just staying here for two nights is bad enough without you adding to the bill!'

'You should have let me book the room as I offered to do, remember? Anyway, you look strung tighter than a virgin's knicker elastic. Why not relax now and let me take over?'

Once more she gave him a brooding look, but it was no good. Once she was near him, in spite of her emotional tangle that threatened to twist her up into knots, her feelings took control.

There was tension too in the taut figure as he strolled lightly over to look out of the big old-fashioned sash window. He pushed the net curtains aside to look down into the busy road beneath him, with the imposing edifice of Harrods not too far away opposite him.

'Why didn't you get a room overlooking the park?' he enquired idly. Sue's chest swelled with indignation.

'I was very lucky to get a room at all! This hotel is very popular with visiting Americans, and as I only booked in for a couple of nights I could hardly expect to be given the equivalent of the bridal suite, now could I?' He ignored her dig at his choice of suite in Monaco; just turned to smile at her, his mouth quirking with amusement. 'Anyway, I like the view this side!' she continued obstinately. 'When one lives in the country all the time it's nice to remind oneself of London's extraordinary architectural mix of styles!'

One eyebrow was raised, but he didn't say any more, just stood watching her with the laughter dying out of his eyes, a man who looked vibrantly, intensely alive, whom she wanted to possess her with a passion that would drive everything that lay between them away so that there would only be the primitive coupling of two bodies thirsting for each other's touch.

The tension was broken by Room Service, and Edwin promptly took charge. Sue just sat back in her chair, her grey eyes watching his every move, until they were once more alone.

Edwin, having refused to allow the waiter to open the bottle of Dom Pérignon, did so now himself with an expertise that showed Sue, as if she didn't already know, that he was quite used to doing it; as if drinking champagne in the early evening was part of a lifestyle he was quite accustomed to. He handed her a fizzing glass, the narrow flute holding the golden liquid, then lifted his own glass in a toast.

'Here's to us!' The brown eyes held the grey ones until she was forced to lift her own glass and sip, then he appeared to relax as he came to sit opposite her. 'Now are you really going to let me handle everything from now on?' Quite demoralised, Sue just nodded. 'Right! Well, although your picture isn't a full-sized copy, it's still going to be too big for one person to handle comfortably in these surroundings, so I think we should be prepared to see a couple, don't you agree?' Once more she just nodded her head.

'I'm fairly sure the whole thing is going to be conducted in that same rather amateurish way that everything else has been handled. In other words I'm not expecting experienced villains! All the same if the going looks like getting rough then I expect you to keep well out of the way. We don't want you getting hurt at this stage of the game, do we?'

'No, Edwin,' she replied meekly, just taking another sip of her champagne, the fizzing drink matching the excitement that was flowing through her own veins. Perhaps she ought to resent this masterful taking of control instead of being overjoyed at his nearness.

'Also I'd prefer to get whoever they are actually in here before we start an undignified scuffle. We don't want the world to know any more about this than we can help, do we?' He seemed to take her acceptance for granted. 'That means dark glasses for you, and something to cover that wonderful bright hair, otherwise they'll run a mile when they recognise you!'

She realised that he was actually excited at the prospect of a showdown, and as she'd already worked all this out for herself, she went over to the dressing-table and held up an olive-green beret to show him before fitting it on so that it almost totally covered her hair. Enormous sunglasses dwarfed the rest of her face. Her dark green skirt, buttoned down one side and figure-hugging with its high waist, complemented the beret, and when it was teamed with her white shirt the whole now added up to someone mysterious and faintly Gallic. She was transformed in fact from a conventionally pretty girl into an enigmatic stranger.

'That's great!' Edwin told her admiringly. 'I would hardly have recognised you myself.' He came to stand close to her, and twitched the beret around a bit while she could feel her heart begin to thump like an express train. 'There!' Before she had any idea of what he was going to do, his lips had closed over hers.

What effort of will it took on her part not to open her mouth under his insistent pressure she hoped he would never find out, but she recognised that if she gave in to his wishes then they were both in danger of exploding into such uncontrolled passion that the whole plan would be put in jeopardy. His lips left hers with the utmost reluctance, as if he was quite aware of what she was feeling. She took the glasses off, quite sure they had misted over under the heat of their combined passion, and rather quickly began to wipe them on the edge of her skirt, but she kept her hair covered, unwilling to disturb his arrangement of her beret, and, picking up her champagne glass again, asked, striving for normality, 'Who do you think will come here, Edwin?' If her voice sounded slightly wobbly and unlike herself he was tactful enough not to comment.

'Des, and someone to help him... Are you scared?'

'A little...' The grey eyes met his honestly enough. 'I think now I'm rather dreading the whole thing.' He held out one of his hands, and she let him take hold of one of hers. Its warmth and strength comforted her.

'Think, my darling, how important this whole thing is to us! You know that as well as I do.'

The trouble was, she did, only too well. Suppose it all went wrong? Perhaps Edwin would get hurt. Unconsciously her fingers tightened their grip on his.

'You need more champagne! Here——' he handed her a sandwich '—you'd better take one of these to act as blotting paper.' He grinned. 'We don't want you so drunk you fall flat on your face when you open the door to them.' His fingers tightened on hers. 'Stop worrying; neither of us will get hurt, I promise!'

'That's a promise you might not be able to keep!' she answered, anxious now that he'd brought her secret fears out into the open. Suppose it wasn't Des at all, but some tough chums whom he'd passed her picture on to once he'd realised it was only her copy?

'I can handle that little rat Des with one hand tied behind my back! Now eat your sandwich and drink your champagne. We haven't got much time left before they're due, and as it's supposed to be business we're handling they should be on time!'

He went on talking to her but her senses wouldn't allow her really to hear his words. She knew he was only talking to comfort her. His voice had sounded really vicious when he was talking about Des. She guessed that if he thought she was still guilty then Des, her so-called partner, was trying to play a dirty trick on her behind her back. Maybe he thought Des had taken her picture out of spite; maybe... She sighed, wishing she didn't have to play this constant guessing game with herself over Edwin's motives.

It seemed to her that they'd hardly had a chance to be themselves ever since they'd first met. First she'd been suspicious of his motives in singling her out, now he was suspicious of her. Every time they met she became more and more conscious of her helplessness as far as he was concerned. It seemed that their destinies were meant to be inextricably entwined, and if that was so then she could only pray that they'd learn to trust each other. Perhaps she was a little Victorian miss at heart after all, because she certainly didn't seem to mind him taking over.

The knock on the door caught her unawares, and her eyes looked both frightened and a little piteous as they rose to meet the warm brown ones.

'It's OK!' he whispered, then, picking up his glass so that there should be no immediate sign that there were two people in the room, he moved forward, so that he would be hidden by the opening door.

Sue's hands were trembling as she put on the dark glasses, then with a conscious effort she opened the door, standing back to allow the two people outside to carry in the picture they were both holding, before she shut it quickly again behind them. Edwin moved in smoothly to stand behind her, one of his hands on her shoulder, and she felt the vibrant shock that ran through his body as he looked at the two people who'd been responsible for so much of their unhappiness.

She took off her beret and sunglasses and shook out the bright, tumbling silk that was her hair, but her eyes were sad as she looked into the two horrified faces.

'Well, well, well.' Edwin's voice sounded light, but with that dangerous edge to it that she'd heard only once before. 'What a surprise!'

CHAPTER EIGHT

GEORGINA turned on Des. 'I told you this was a mistake! Just because you're so greedy, you have to try and make a deal on everything!' she yelled.

'I see, so you're going to try and blame me, are you? I should have guessed you'd try on something like that, but it won't work, sunshine! Your boss now knows who set up this little deal!' His nasal voice now deteriorated into a cockney whine. 'You ain't going to be able to wriggle out of this one, lovely!'

'Shut up, shut up, you idiot!' Georgina's voice had now risen almost to a scream. She too had been wearing dark glasses, and her hair was hidden under a nondescript hat. Des in total contrast had remained as he always was: black leather jacket and matching trousers were perhaps a step up on his usual jeans, but he still looked a wide boy; his whole countenance was concentrated on watching every shift of expression on Sue's face as he looked for possible escape.

Her picture appeared to be covered in some sort of man-made fabric used for light luggage. Although there were zips around the edges, indicating it was some sort of case, it hardly looked a particularly safe way of transporting a large canvas around.

It was Edwin's turn to assert himself. 'I'll take charge of that if you don't mind!' He laid the picture to rest on the large double bed, then turned back to Georgina and Des, his face unreadable.

'Now...' He focused a hard-eyed stare on Georgina. 'Perhaps you'd be good enough to tell me how you found out that Sue's home was empty the night of my party, and, more importantly, how you knew about her pictures!'

She gave him a sulky look. 'It wasn't difficult. I sent out the invitations, remember?'

'Yes?'

There was a distinctly menacing look on his face, and Georgina retreated from it. 'I went through your private files...'

'Did you indeed? I should have thought you'd been brought up to know better!' This damning indictment, or the expression on his face, shut her up. 'I take it that you both think you're going to walk away from this little episode unscathed?' The biting sarcasm in his voice made Georgina wince. 'How many times have you used my gallery to transport stolen pictures abroad?'

'Never! And I'm not a thief! There was never any intention of selling those Tamertons!'

'This, I take it, doesn't count?' Once more his sarcasm brought sharp colour to her pale cheeks.

'Well, it isn't of any real value, is it?' she sneered. 'Only a copy, worth maybe a thousand or two at best...'

'So why was it offered to Cécile Tamerton as a genuine copy by the artist of his own work?'

'B-but it wasn't!' she stammered. 'It was offered as a copy. Des wanted to make something for expenses...'

Edwin's biting gaze switched to the younger man. Des met Edwin's eyes quickly, before going back to watching Sue, and it was at her he looked though he was answering Edwin.

'Sue wouldn't let me come to her house. Thought I wasn't good enough for her! I could have told her about others better born than her...'

But Sue had had enough. What was the point in letting him go on and belittle Georgina's pride? Because that was what he wanted to do.

'That's enough, Des!' She turned to Edwin. 'Don't let him go on, he's only trying to humiliate...' She nodded her head in Georgina's direction. 'Anyway, I'm not interested in a prosecution, not now I've got my pictures back!'

Des tried to continue, but Edwin cut him off savagely. 'Shut up! If you don't want me to speak to your boss about this then you'd better be prepared to keep your mouth shut. I could make sure everyone finds out about this particular little caper. That wouldn't do you much good in the trade, and if you think I'd keep my mouth closed for Georgina Foliot's sake then you're wrong!'

Des suddenly looked white and shaken, as if he had been sure of exactly that.

'Now get out!' Edwin continued. 'I'm going to keep my eye on you, and if I ever hear you might be mixed up in anything remotely crooked again then you can bet I'll make quite certain you never work in the antiques field again!'

Des, looking shattered, turned on his heel and left, not even bothering to give Georgina anything but the briefest of glances before the door closed behind him.

Edwin then turned his attention to his assistant. 'You're fired as from today!' he told her cruelly.

'Don't try to come back to the gallery. Anything of yours will be sent on to you, and don't even ask me for a reference. The same rules apply to you! Get mixed up in anything like this again and I'll make sure everyone hears what you attempted over Sue's pictures...'

'I'm not a thief!' she protested, but he overruled her.

'Oh, yes, you are, my dear. Devious, dishonest, as well as dishonourable! And if I hear that you've been causing trouble for either of us by gossiping, or trying to give your version of events, I'll personally inform your father of your activities. I don't think he'd take kindly to hearing that his only daughter was mixed up with rough trade, do you?' The distaste in his voice made it clear what he thought and felt about her.

For one awful moment Georgina's poise cracked and Sue thought she was going to break down and cry in front of them; then she pulled herself together, and with one last malevolent glare at Sue she left the room.

Feeling weak at the knees, Sue collapsed into one of the chairs. 'Thank God that's over!' she told Edwin with heartfelt gratitude, then leaned forward to pick up her glass, trying to think of a suitable toast that would break the ice between them. He was standing ramrod-straight, half turned away from her, and she realised that he was furiously angry.

She put her glass down and came to stand next to him. 'I'm sorry you had to find out about her the hard way...' Her voice was gentle.

'You're sorry!' He turned to face her and she saw that he was in a flaming temper. 'My God! I'm the one who owes you an apology, and don't think I don't know it!'

'Don't, Edwin! I know——'

'I would never have told her about your pictures; that was too personal, too important to me even then to share it with her! My God! She's a two-faced, double-dealing bitch and she deserves to suffer for what she's done to us!'

'She was in love with you, Edwin! I think she lost her head through jealousy, because she could see right from the start that you were intrigued by me! Didn't you guess at all that she was fond of you?'

A flushed warmed his skin. 'No, I bloody didn't! Just because she was good at her job... She never had the slightest reason to suppose I was ever interested in her!'

'How sad!' Sue answered softly.

'For heaven's sake, don't go feeling sorry for her now!' Edwin sounded goaded beyond all reason.

Sue gave him a clear look from limpid grey eyes. 'How can I not? I think she loved you, and hoped I'd be so suspicious of you after the theft of my pictures that I'd end whatever it was that had started between us...'

He pulled her savagely into his arms, then, holding her hard against his lean strength, said, 'But nothing can do that, can it, my love? Whatever suspicions we both had about each other were never enough to kill our need for each other, were they?'

'No...' she whispered, her eyes glinting up at his face through half-closed lids. His mouth claimed hers with a fierce possessiveness which she made no attempt to fight. She clung to him, moulding her softness against the hard contours of his superbly fit body with erotic pleasure.

He took his lips from hers, and both hands gently cupped her face as she slowly opened her eyes to see for herself just what she had achieved. The light brown eyes were lit with a fierce flame, his nostrils flared with desire.

'You did say you'd booked this room for two nights?' The brown eyes now held a glint of amusement.

'I did indeed,' she breathed, hardly daring to hope what he was suggesting.

'Then it would be a pity to waste it, wouldn't it?' His voice was husky and low, yet she caught the edge in it of a man driven almost beyond the point of control.

'It certainly would...' She watched with amusement as Edwin, momentarily abandoning her, flipped the 'Do Not Disturb' sign on to the outside of the door, then returned to remove her picture from its resting place on the bed before making short work of the bedcover. He tossed off the jacket of his suit before refilling their two glasses and coming back to join her.

'We've all the time in the world, my beautiful darling!' He toasted her with his eyes, which seemed to her over-heated imagination to take on the same qualities as the champagne as they burned with a sparkling golden light, but when she responded, her eyes laughing back at him, he seemed to become possessed with an urgency that had little to do with his earlier statement about having all the time in the world.

Both glasses were hurriedly put down as his lips once again possessed hers, and this time his hands were not decorously around her face, but exploring her body with a hot urgency that brought its own excitement in their wake. Expertly, but slowly, as if savouring every moment, he began to remove her clothes, and as she felt his hands on her skin she erupted with a passion that was as surprising to her as perhaps it was to Edwin.

He removed her bra with hands that shook slightly, then as his mouth found one hardened nipple she moaned with surprise and shock. His hands and mouth smoothed and caressed until she was ready to yield in sensuous torment.

'Edwin, please...please...' It seemed as if he knew what she needed so desperately.

'Undress me...' His voice took on a low, passionate note, his eyes already clouded with desire as they met her feverishly bright ones. Her fingers fumbled clumsily with the buttons of his shirt as he lay back and watched her with hooded eyes as slowly she exposed his hot, bare skin. He groaned as she lifted herself on to him, pressing her naked skin to his, and as their mouths met with a passionate, aching tenderness his hands slowly explored lower, removing her brief panties, until, driven half mad, she wriggled away to continue her work of undressing him. But it seemed this time that he did not have the patience to wait, as he swiftly helped her to remove the rest of his clothes.

His hands continued to explore the more private areas of her body confidently, and as their expert touch presaged more sensuous stroking she began to tremble in his arms.

Swiftly one knee parted her thighs, as he half lay over her, his face mirroring the flush of desire that threatened to burn her up unless he gave her the longed-for release that she pleaded for so mindlessly. 'Please, oh, please, Edwin...!'

Just before he entered her, his mouth took fierce possession, his tongue exploring deeply as her body welcomed his thrusting manhood with delicious rhythmic appreciation. Their joint physical desire brought them together quickly, almost too quickly, in explosive abandonment. Shaken with a shuddering delight of such magnitude that she felt as if Edwin had set off a spectacular display of fireworks inside her, Sue allowed her body to collapse into fluid acquiescence under his controlling forcefulness, hardly aware of the strange little cries she gave. So fierce and so devastating an assault on her body left her trembling and shaking in his arms, and it was some time before she realised that he too was shaking in the aftermath of spent passion.

They lay together in languid ease, neither of them yet capable of saying or doing anything, so traumatic had been their first experience of each other's bodies. Indeed Sue's mind was full of a quiet amazement. Justin had been her only other lover, yet her experience just now with Edwin was light-years away from anything she had enjoyed with him.

Edwin rolled her towards him, so that she could see the possessive, lazy amusement in his eyes. Yet there was also a suspicion of awe, as if he still couldn't quite believe what had happened between them. She stretched, lazily, like a cat, then allowed her mouth to tilt into the promise of a smile. 'Wow!' was all she said, but it was enough.

He pulled her into his arms, cradling her against his chest, while his mouth covered her hair with light kisses. 'Never, my little darling...' even his voice sounded off-balance and a little wobbly '...has the reality so exceeded the dreams! What are you, some kind of witch?'

Her hands were doing their own stroking, exploring. She felt possessive, and gloried in her ability to make him behave with such passionate abandon.

'Maybe,' she teased, 'I've put a spell on you!'

'I'm not complaining, oh, no! You can put as many spells on me as you like.'

'Do you want me to turn you into a toad?' She leant on her elbow to look up at him, pretended surprise on her face.

'You can turn me inside out if you like!' he teased in return. She pretended to consider, then shook her head, laughing down at him.

'No... I think I like you best as you are after all!' She pressed a rain of little kisses all over his chest, until with a groan he stopped her, forcing her lips to meet his once more. They drank deeply of each other, as if even now they still couldn't have enough of each other, as if they needed more.

And so they made love again, a gentler coming together this time, but still as deeply passionate. He took her to the heights with his sensuous eroticism while she abandoned all pretence of being anything but a willing pupil under his tutelage. It was as if he released her somehow, gave her the ability to fly to the stars, soaring ever higher on heights of ecstasy she'd never even dreamed she was capable of. That she had the power to please him equally became her most important goal. He too must be free to roam the universe at her side, two souls joined in a spiritual union greater than any physical union of their bodies.

They slept, then awoke to discover that they were both ravenously hungry.

'Room Service, don't you think?' Edwin teased. 'I don't want to get dressed again this evening, do you?'

'You know I don't!' Her grey eyes were brilliant with a light he'd never seen before. For decency's sake, she tidied their clothes, and Edwin insisted on both of them having a shower together, so she discovered the intimate pleasure of soaping his body, while he did the same for her. There was a great deal of laughter and giggles, but they both appeared sober enough in their white towelling robes when the meal Edwin had chosen for them arrived.

Alone once more, he insisted she sat on his knee while he fed her oysters.

'Food for the gods, my darling! Anyway, they're supposed to be an aphrodisiac...'

'You think I need help?' she pouted, in mock-anger.

'Oh, no, not you...' His eyes were once more giving her messages that had the blood running swiftly through her veins, and the sexual excitement they generated in each other was already beginning to raise the temperature. This time, though, they seemed prepared to wait, as if they knew that by doing so they'd heighten their pleasure together.

Edwin had chosen guinea-fowl, roasted quite simply, but with an accompanying sauce of mushrooms and herbs. He still continued to feed her, as if she were a baby, and, content at their closeness, she allowed him to do so, laughing at his jokes; but she was discovering another appetite, one more powerful than food, a driving carnal urge that it seemed he shared. He'd chosen a Pouilly-Fumé, a dry, slightly smoky white wine that tasted delicious, for them to drink, and for pudding he'd chosen a rich *crème brûlée*, topped with fruit; but after one spoonful she shook her head.

'No more?' he teased. 'Or are you frightened of getting fat?' One hand slid intimately between her robe. 'I don't think you need worry; I like your curves...'

Already her breasts had hardened under his caress, so sensitised at his lightest touch that she caught her breath, her head dropping back as her mouth half parted, her eyes closed.

'Dear God! You drive me wild! Am I never to have any peace from you?' he growled.

'Never!' she whispered, but she was already aware of the leaping life that surged against her body as she parted his robe, eager to feel his hot skin pressed next to hers yet again. His tongue began to trace an erotic path over her body as she shivered in delighted anticipation of what was to come.

'My lovely...' Edwin raised his head to look down at her, all rosy and flushed, and she entwined two white arms around him, drawing him down on to her soft curves, and his mouth parted in a smile, as he allowed himself to yield again to her impatient demands.

* * *

'I suppose you know your own mind best, but Sue, don't you think the two of you should have this out?' Bridget looked at the girl in front of her, a worried frown on her face. 'For the last two months the two of you have been mixed up in, according to you, the most passionate affair this century! Yet you're still not totally sure that he loves you! I'd have thought it was a pretty foregone conclusion myself, but if ever a girl had to doubt happiness handed to her on a plate it's you!'

'But I explained to you, Bridget! I think he's just hooked on the whole Victorian thing, and I'm part of it. I'm not sure he really loves me as a person!'

Bridget made a rude noise. 'Personally I think that sounds a load of rubbish! I'm accusing you of doubting your chance of happiness! Just because your affair with Justin went wrong because of his mother— for which, I have to say, you should be thankful— you now seem to doubt that you're good enough for Edwin. If I were you I'd leave him to be the judge of that, dear!'

'That's just it!' Sue wailed. 'I have! And look where we are—nothing has changed!'

'Don't you think he might be taking it slow for your sake? What is he, six or seven years older than you?'

'Seven, but Georgina told me he'd had hundreds of girlfriends in the past!' she accused.

'So? Far better that he should get them out of his system,' Bridget answered robustly. 'Better than having them after he's married...'

'I don't know that he's even considered marriage.' Sue's whole pose spoke of her sadness, her doubts.

Georgina's lightly spoken words at the party had succeeded in poisoning her belief in herself.

Bridget gave a sigh. 'For heaven's sake! He's run off his feet trying to organise his retrospective, find a replacement for Georgina, and, according to you, conduct the greatest love-affair this century! Give him a chance, Sue! Anyway, how do you know he hasn't got something special planned when you meet in London tomorrow?'

'He has, he wants to show me around his exhibits!' she replied waspishly. 'Oh, I don't know... Sometimes I wish I could read his mind; that I could be sure he loves me!'

'Why go looking for trouble? I know I'm only an old woman you never listen to, but I think he absolutely adores you, and underneath all this fuss you're making I think you know it!'

'I know he fancies me, but that's not enough, is it?'

'It sounds like quite enough to be going on with! For heaven's sake, you haven't even known each other six months yet!'

'Time doesn't matter in something like this; you either know or you don't!'

'Well, I can see there's no point in arguing with you any more, dear, because you seem to have made your mind up! To change the subject, have you thought about the practicalities of keeping on this house?'

'Well, no, I haven't; how could I with all this going on?' Sue threw her arms in the air.

'That'll give you the perfect chance to bring up the subject with Edwin, won't it? I don't think he's happy about you living down here all alone!'

'He hasn't said anything about it!'

'He's probably had his mind fixed on more immediate matters!' Bridget teased, before she left. 'If ever there was a girl more determined to look a gift horse in the mouth, it's you! And, what's more, you were just the same as a child! Couldn't believe you were happy until you were told so!' She banged the kitchen door shut behind her and walked back home muttering all the way.

'Well, darling, what do you think?' Edwin pulled her next to him as they both stood back and stared critically at the picture of the girl with the two goats which took pride of place in his gallery.

'It looks wonderful, Edwin! You've had it cleaned.' He dropped a kiss on to her hair.

'You don't mind, do you?'

'No, why should I?' She returned his kiss with enthusiasm. 'Where are you hanging the others?'

'Come and see...' She followed him downstairs, and there, in a small room all to themselves, were the four pictures which even Edwin now admitted were probably painted by Augustus Frome. Newly framed, they hung splendidly in all their glory, and Sue's eyes misted over with tears.

'I wish Gran could have seen this! I know this was what she wanted most of all.'

'I wish she could as well. It seems a shame that she didn't quite have enough courage to tell the world about him sooner.'

'I don't know, maybe she was right to leave it until Victorian art had become fashionable again! I mean, if she'd spoken earlier in her life, how many people would have noticed or even cared? But now, thanks to you, everyone is going to know about him!'

'Sadly, there's pathetically little to find out. It was a tragedy he died so young; he was remarkably talented and I think would have gone on to make quite a name for himself when he discovered his own style.'

Sue sighed. 'I'm sure Gran was in love with him! That's why she kept his pictures so close to her. I wonder if there are any more?'

Edwin shook his head. 'Somehow I rather doubt it. I've seen a great number of Tamertons, and none of them particularly shows his hand. I wonder if John Tamerton himself knew how very good Frome was?'

'I think he must have known, otherwise he wouldn't have trusted him to finish off that last large painting, would he? I mean, I know his sight was going by then, something that he was desperately keen no one should find out, but he must have known how much potential talent Augustus had when he first took him on as a pupil. He probably even knew that he didn't have long to live. Consumption was after all relatively common then, wasn't it?'

'Yes, sadly it was. No wonder really the Victorians were so obsessed with death. It was all around them; a part of life that we find difficult to understand today, certainly in this part of the world.'

Sue clung close to him, as if talk of death was not something she wished personally to consider at this moment in time. He looked down at her shining head and gave a tender smile.

'Let's go home, shall we? Tomorrow's going to be a long and busy day, so we might as well relax and go to bed early tonight.'

She slanted up at him one of her glancing looks, knowing he found their occasional enforced separations an intolerable strain. Also it was useless to pretend that she was happy apart from him either. So far the physical part of their relationship had been so powerful that she guessed he'd been unable to consider anything really apart from the driving need to be together as much as possible.

She tried to rationalise with herself that this stage in their relationship had to ease to allow true love to grow between them, but in particular she was still worried by Edwin's total physical enthralment with her body. She was still frightened that apart from sex somehow she didn't quite measure up to those hidden standards he seemed to have. She'd tried to express these fears rather unsatisfactorily to Bridget, who hadn't seemed to understand at all.

For the moment Edwin seemed content trying to ensure their physical satisfaction to the exclusion of everything else. They talked, yes, but it seemed to Sue that their communication was so overshadowed by that continual unspoken dialogue between them that it had an air of unreality.

Edwin's total silence about where their relationship was going had undermined her security, and she was becoming afraid that he never would mention it, that once more she was going to be found wanting. Just lately she had found that her unspoken fears were beginning to affect her when they made love; that somehow she was unable to give him the totally uninhibited response he was used to. She didn't know if he was aware of this or not, or whether, totally immersed in his own pleasure, he had become a little uncaring of hers.

Tomorrow would be the start of his major retrospective of late Victorian art, featuring John Tamerton, and, apart from the unknown Augustus Frome, two other artists of a similar standing. He'd taken on a girl to replace Georgina who'd been working in one of the major auction houses in the Victorian art department for several years. Apart from being knowledgeable she was very nice, and Sue thought she was a great improvement on the snooty Georgina. It helped that she was married, a young bride in fact, and therefore no threat to her.

She'd come up from Devon that day specially for the opening party Edwin was giving in the gallery tomorrow. He'd insisted that she had to be present, and she had been more than happy to comply with his wishes. They were going to go back to his flat, where they'd be alone for the first time since the week before last, and she knew he was impatient to have her to himself.

His apartment was in, appropriately enough, an old Victorian block in Pimlico. Large and surprisingly light, it was luxurious without being oppressively so. Sue had come to realise that he must be a very rich man, although they never talked about money, and this too added to her growing feelings of insecurity.

How was she to be expected to live up to his expectations apart from her looks? Maybe the time had come for a showdown between them, yet that thought terrified her. Suppose he was happy for things to continue as they were? And she couldn't deny that he'd given her greater pleasure than she'd ever dreamed of, so would she have the strength to put that at risk by querying their relationship?

Edwin insisted on cooking supper in the kitchen for them. She was allowed only to toss the salad, which his daily had already washed and prepared and left in the crisper department in the fridge. He was frying large Dublin Bay prawns in butter and garlic, which looked and smelt delicious. She had soon discovered that he had a passion for all kinds of fish.

He filled her in on all the latest gossip, making her laugh, but it seemed he sensed she wasn't truly relaxed. Over coffee, which they had sitting on one of two enormous red brocade sofas that dominated his drawing-room, he turned her face towards him.

'What is it, Sue?' Her eyes met his, a little frightened; she hadn't realised he'd been aware of the problems. 'What's wrong?' Was that a hint of fear in his eyes? No, that had to be her imagination. She shrugged her shoulders in sudden helplessness, her eyes filling with tears. He took hold of her shoulders in a sort of passion. 'Tell me!'

'I—oh, Edwin! It's so difficult...'

'Are you trying to tell me it's finished between us? Is that it?' His fingers had tightened uncomfortably on her shoulders.

'No, no!' She saw his growing frown. 'Please, please don't get cross with me!'

He saw her fear, and a bewildered expression crossed his face, as if he couldn't work out what could possibly be troubling her. 'Don't you know by now that I love you? That I'd never do anything willingly to make you unhappy?'

She looked at him with surprise. 'You love me?'

Once more he took hold of her shoulders and gave her a little shake. 'How could you doubt it? Do you think what we share is nothing out of the ordinary? Don't you know this is what most people dream of discovering, but few ever do?'

She looked back at him, half believing, yet not quite daring to give up the last of her fears. 'You really love me? I thought that after all perhaps I didn't quite live up to your image of that little girl who grew up to be my grandmother...'

He looked at her in total astonishment.

'But I've told you! Countless times——'

She interrupted quietly, rather sadly, 'You've never told me before that you love me!'

'I never have? I think you must be mistaken. Anyway, don't you know by now that actions speak louder than words?' He picked up one of her hands and placed a kiss in her palm, closing her fingers over it, as if by doing so she could keep it forever. 'I thought I'd shown you in every way a man can that I love you this side of madness!' He looked deep into her eyes. 'God knows where you picked up these feelings of inferiority...' He picked up her other hand, and pressed a kiss into that palm, his eyes all the time holding hers. 'How could you have thought I only loved you as an image? Yes, of course you interested me initially because of your likeness to your grandmother as a young girl, but I'm upset that you should consider me such a shallow man that I should only have been capable of falling in love with something so ephemeral.'

His grip on her hand tightened. 'You're not only beautiful, you're brave and courageous as well. I'm not surprised your friends all love you, because you're fun to be with. Also you have an enviable talent for being able to re-create masterpieces, and I cannot imagine my life without you!' The fierce intensity of his voice, his conviction, began to have an effect on her feelings. Dared she really begin to hope?

'This evening I was going to propose to you. I would have done it a long time ago, but I didn't think it was fair to rush you off your feet. I always knew my own mind, but I wasn't sure about you. When sex is as good as it is with us, sometimes it's difficult to look beyond it. Because, my darling, never confuse sex with love! I always knew you weren't experienced, that you hadn't slept around, but I didn't want to take unfair advantage of you.' He was silent for a moment, then his voice was low as he said, 'If you'll have me, I want to be your husband. I want it more than anything in this world, or beyond!' The passionate conviction and intensity of his voice moved her almost to tears.

He put his hand in his pocket and drew out a small box, which he opened. Sue's last doubts went skittering away in a burst of such happiness that she felt radiant with joy. Here was no old-fashioned ring in a Victorian setting. A single solitaire diamond, set uncompromisingly in platinum, was as modern a setting as she could have wished for. Edwin smiled. 'I hope it fits!' He slipped it over her finger while she gazed at it, open-mouthed with happiness. 'I thought we'd announce our engagement tomorrow at the party. What do you think?'

'Oh, Edwin!' She threw her arms around his neck. 'I love you, I love you! Why didn't you do this before?'

'I wasn't sure you'd have me!' he teased.

'Really?' Her big grey eyes looked back into his, mirroring his great love for her.

'Really and truly!' he answered.

'But I was so afraid you didn't really care! That this was only an affair for you!'

'My beloved idiot! I never thought you a fool before!' His voice caressed her.

'And I can return the compliment! I fell in love with you almost as soon as I first saw you in one of those awful auction rooms! Well,' she amended, 'I didn't know it at the time maybe, but I did!'

'Love at first sight?' he teased.

'Why not?' Sue looked down at the ring on her finger. 'You know, this is absolutely beautiful, and I didn't thank you for it!' She reached up to kiss him. 'We'll be very happy together, won't we?' she whispered shyly into his ear.

'It won't be my fault if we're not!' he responded, then proceeded to deepen her kiss into one of passion; and now, secure in his arms, she responded enthusiastically to this latest assault on her person.

MILLS & BOON

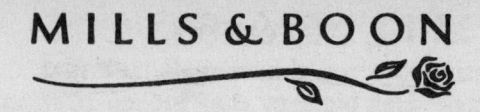

HEARTS OF FIRE by Miranda Lee

Welcome to our compelling family saga set in the glamorous world of opal dealing in Australia. Laden with dark secrets, forbidden desires and scandalous discoveries, **Hearts of Fire** unfolds over a series of 6 books, but each book also features a passionate romance with a happy ending and can be read independently.

Book 1: SEDUCTION & SACRIFICE
Published: April 1994   *FREE* with Book 2

WATCH OUT for special promotions!

Lenore had loved Zachary Marsden secretly for years. Loyal, handsome and protective, Zachary was the perfect husband. Only Zachary would never leave his wife... would he?

Book 2: DESIRE & DECEPTION
Published: April 1994   Price £2.50

Jade had a name for Kyle Armstrong: *Mr Cool*. He was the new marketing manager at Whitmore Opals—the job *she* coveted. However, the more she tried to hate this usurper, the more she found him attractive...

Book 3: PASSION & THE PAST
Published: May 1994   Price £2.50

Melanie was intensely attracted to Royce Grantham—which shocked her! She'd been so sure after the tragic end of her marriage that she would never feel for any man again. How strong was her resolve not to repeat past mistakes?

MILLS & BOON

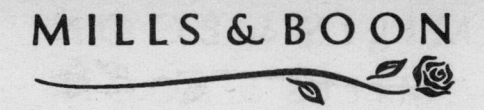

HEARTS OF FIRE by Miranda Lee

Book 4: FANTASIES & THE FUTURE
Published: June 1994   Price £2.50

The man who came to mow the lawns was more stunning than any of Ava's fantasies, though she realised that Vincent Morelli thought she was just another rich, lonely housewife looking for excitement! But, Ava knew that her narrow, boring existence was gone forever...

Book 5: SCANDALS & SECRETS
Published: July 1994   Price £2.50

Celeste Campbell had lived on her hatred of Byron Whitmore for twenty years. Revenge was sweet...until news reached her that Byron was considering remarriage. Suddenly she found she could no longer deny all those long-buried feelings for him...

Book 6: MARRIAGE & MIRACLES
Published: August 1994   Price £2.50

Gemma's relationship with Nathan was in tatters, but her love for him remained intact—she was going to win him back! Gemma knew that Nathan's terrible past had turned his heart to stone, and she was asking for a miracle. But it was possible that one could happen, wasn't it?

Don't miss all six books!

Available from WH Smith, John Menzies, Volume One, Forbuoys, Martins, Woolworths, Tesco, Asda, Safeway and other paperback stockists.
Also available from Mills & Boon Reader Service, FREEPOST,
PO Box 236, Croydon, Surrey CR9 9EL (UK Postage & Packing free).

MILLS & BOON

Proudly present...

CHARLOTTE LAMB'S ♥ *100th* ♥ ROMANCE

This is a remarkable achievement for a writer who had her first Mills & Boon novel published in 1973. Some six million words later and with sales around the world, her novels continue to be popular with romance fans everywhere.

Her centenary romance *'VAMPIRE LOVER'* is a suspense-filled story of dark desires and tangled emotions—Charlotte Lamb at her very best.

Published: June 1994   Price: £1.90

Available from WH Smith, John Menzies, Volume One, Forbuoys, Martins, Woolworths, Tesco, Asda, Safeway and other paperback stockists. Also available from Mills & Boon Reader Service, FREEPOST, PO Box 236, Croydon, Surrey CR9 9EL (UK Postage & Packing free).

HEART ⚭ HEART

Win a year's supply of Romances
ABSOLUTELY FREE?

Yes, you can win one whole year's supply of Mills & Boon Romances. It's easy! Find a path through the maze, starting at the top left square and finishing at the bottom right.

The symbols must follow the sequence above.

You can move up, down, left, right and diagonally.

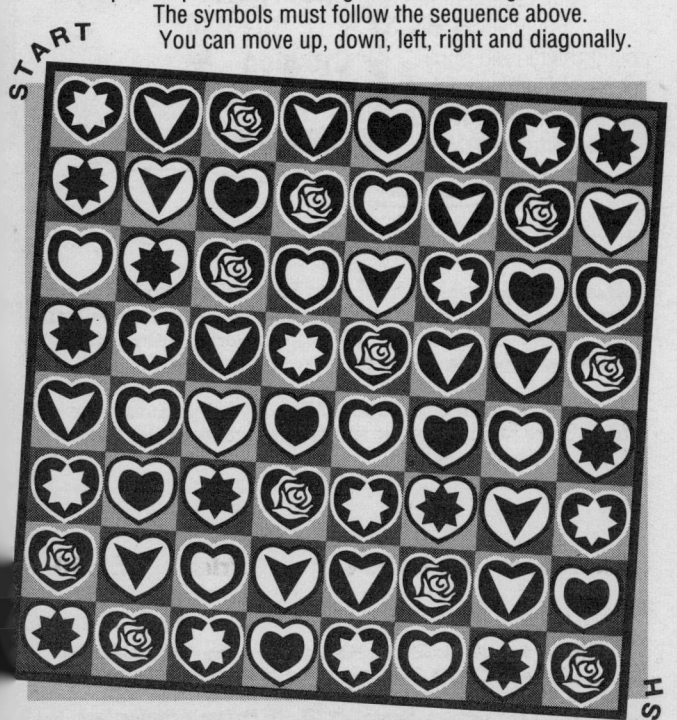

START

FINISH

Please turn over for entry details

HEART TO HEART

SEND YOUR ENTRY NOW!

The first five correct entries picked out of the bag after the closing date will each win one year's supply of Mills & Boon Romances (six books every month for twelve months - worth over £85).
What could be easier?

Don't forget to enter your name and address in the space below then put this page in an envelope and post it today (you don't need a stamp).
Competition closes 31st November 1994.

HEART TO HEART Competition
FREEPOST
P.O. Box 236
Croydon
Surrey CR9 9EL

Are you a Reader Service subscriber?   Yes ☐   No ☐

Ms/Mrs/Miss/Mr _____ COMHH

Address _____

_____

_____

Postcode _____

Signature _____

One application per household. Offer valid only in U.K. and Eire. You may be mailed with offers from other reputable companies as a result of this application. Please tick box if you would prefer not to receive such offers. ☐

mps MAILING PREFERENCE SERVICE